STEᵖ 12
BROTHER
with Benefits

SECOND SEASON

MIA CLARK

Stepbrother With Benefits 12 is a work of fiction. Names, characters, places, and incidents either are the product of the author's imagination or are used fictitiously. Any resemblance to actual persons, living or dead, events, or locales is entirely coincidental.

ISBN: 1517394279
ISBN-13: 978-1517394271

Book design by Cerys du Lys
Cover design by Cerys du Lys
Cover Image © Depositphotos | avgustino

Cherrylily.com

DEDICATION

Thank you to Ethan and Cerys for helping me with this book and everything involved in the process. This is a dream come true and I wouldn't have been able to do it without them. Thank you, thank you!

CONTENTS

ACKNOWLEDGMENTS

Thank you for taking a chance on my book!

I know that the stepbrother theme can be a difficult one to deal with for a lot of people for a variety of reasons, and so I took that into consideration when I was writing this. While this is a story about forbidden love, it's also a story about two people becoming friends, too. Sometimes you need someone to push you in your life, even when you think everything is fine. Sometimes you need someone to be there, even when you don't know how to ask them to stay with you.

This is that kind of story. It is about two people becoming friends, and then becoming lovers. The forbidden aspects add tension, but it's more than that, too. Sometimes opposites attract in the best way possible. I hope you enjoy my books!

STEPBROTHER WITH BENEFITS

1 - Ethan

ALRIGHT, LOOK, I'M SLEEPING. I'm dreaming about something. I don't know what the fuck it is. Bears maybe, or wolves, or dogs that look like wolves, or wolves that are dogs that are actually bears but really they're aliens.

Or blowjobs.

You might not think any of that shit is connected, but let me assure you that blowjobs are always relevant to everything. Yeah, alright, so if you're lost in the woods and about to get eaten by a wolf, a blowjob isn't exactly going to save you, but it's sure going to make you feel a hell of a lot better and that's what's important.

Sometimes you just need to lean back and calm the fuck down. Getting a blowjob is a great way to do that.

I'm pretty fucking sure I'm dreaming about blowjobs now. Yeah, so, I'm asleep, and I don't know how I know anything, but I feel like it's easy to picture Ashley's perfect as fuck lips wrapping around my cock. I love the way she looks up at me when she's about to do it, like she's excited but a little nervous, too. She licks her lips and then pulls her bottom lip into her mouth, biting down on it slightly before teasing out her tongue and licking at the tip of my cock, and...

"Hey! You two, wake up and get out here. We need to talk."

Holy fucking shit. Are you for real? I'm having a dream about blowjobs over here, and not only that but Ashley's blowjobs. I am the recipient of these blowjobs, and I better fucking be the only recipient ever.

Except, yeah, so that's my dad and now I'm not dreaming anymore because he's loud as fuck and I'm definitely awake.

I've got an erection, though. I guess I've got that going for me, for whatever the fuck that's worth. I don't think it's worth a lot because I've got to get up and get out of the tent instead of doing something more productive with my cock.

I feel like Ashley has the same idea, too. We're on the same level here, of the same mindset. She's awake, too, and blinking her big beautiful eyes at me while sneaking glances downwards at the throbbing piece of art between my legs.

Yeah, I just called my cock a piece of art. Do you have a problem with that?

She reaches out and grabs my cock, teasing and stroking me with her hand. "I wish I could make you cum right now," she says, whispering to me.

Yeah, you know what, Princess? I wish you could, too. I really fucking wish you could...

"No screwing around!" my dad says, loud.

Yeah? You know what? You know fucking what, Dad?

Fuck you.

I'm going to screw around.

Quick and fast as fuck, I grab Ashley's wrist and pull her hand away from my cock. She looks at me, confused and surprised for a second, but that's all I give her. One second, baby girl, you'll realize what's up after that. I pin her hand above her head and roll her onto her back and then slide on top of her.

I'm ready, and I'm pretty fucking sure she's ready, but I guess we're about to find out.

I slide her legs apart with my knee and then use my free hand to guide myself towards her delicious as fuck pussy. I'm feeling really vulgar right now, which I guess I'm going to blame on being rudely awakened by my dad and told not to screw around.

I push my hips forward and slide my way right inside of her. She's wet and ready for me and it only takes a fraction of a second for me to go deep inside of her, my balls slamming against her body. Her eyes roll into the back of her head and she opens her mouth to let out a moan. I press my lips to hers, stopping her from giving us away.

I'm screwing around here, Princess. Don't ruin this for me.

"You still wish you could make me cum right now?" I whisper into her ear.

"Ethan, your dad..." she gasps, hushed.

I grind my body against hers. I can't be as loud as I want, because, yeah, my dad's right outside, but I can still enjoy myself, and I'm pretty sure she's going to enjoy this, too. I slide against her clit and her eyes roll into the back of her head again. Aw, fuck, that's gorgeous.

I love the way she reacts to me. It's not just about this, not just about sex or lust or whatever the fuck, it's just everything. She looks so perfect when I'm with her, like she's finally able to be herself, and I feel like I can be myself, too.

"You tell me what to do, Princess," I say. "My dad can wait. This is about you and me, alright?"

"Ethan..." she whimpers, refusing to answer.

The look on her face says it all. She's trapped between being the good girl and giving in to her naughty side. Oh, how I want her to give in. The struggle is real right here, and it's turning me on even more. My cock pulses and throbs inside her. I ease out a little, then push back in, rocking my hips against her sexy fucking body.

My dad's sitting by the campfire spot, grumbling.

My stepmom murmurs to him. "Oh, let them sleep a little. I'm sure they're both tired, and it's the summer. Not everyone is used to getting up as early as you, honey."

"You hear that, Princess," I whisper to her. "We've got time."

"Ethan, it's just..." She buries her face in my shoulder. Holy fuck, it's cute and sexy at the same time. Why are you doing this to me, Princess?

"Yeah, what is it?" I ask her, grinning.

"They're right outside!" she hisses, almost laughing. "It's weird."

"Listen," I tell her. "I'm making up a new rule. What the fuck rule are we on now?"

"Twenty-one," she says. "But do you really think this is a good time for rules?"

"Yeah, it's the fucking best time," I say. "Here's the rule. Rule twenty-one. I'll always be there when you need me, Princess. No matter what you need, I'm here for you."

She stares at me for a second, really trying not to laugh now. The huge grin on her face is contagious and I start to grin, too. I kiss her fast and she kisses me back and we're both just fucking grinning and trying not to laugh because I'm balls deep inside her and our parents are right outside our tent, so, uh... yeah, what the fuck are we doing?

I'm kind of a bad boy, though. I can get away with this kind of stuff. It's just what I do, you know?

"You'll always be there for me?" she asks, giggling a little. "That's not really a rule, is it?"

"Nah, the rule is that I have to be there, I guess," I tell her. "I don't know. Why are you making this difficult?"

"You realize you just made this rule so that you can have an excuse to do very naughty sexy things, right?"

"Yeah, so?"

"I'm just making sure we're both on the same page," she whispers.

"I think we've always been on the same page, Princess," I say, pulling out of her a little and then pushing back in hard.

She squeezes her arms around my back and makes a face that can only be described as "sexy as fuck I want to fuck the shit out of this girl so bad."

"So... if I say I really want you to cum... I really really want you to cum... then you'll do it because you'll always be here for me no matter what I need?" she asks, whispering right into my ear, sultry, her breath warm and her words hot.

"Yeah," I say. "Exactly."

She licks at my earlobe, sending shivers through my body. Holy fuck, that's nice... yeah, I love you, too, Princess.

"I want you to cum..." she says.

I'm ready. I'm so fucking ready, you don't even know. I pull out and slide back into her, building up a rhythm, prepared to give her exactly what she wants and needs.

"I really want you to cum so bad, Ethan," she says, whimpering and pleading with me.

"Oh, I'm going to cum," I whisper to her, harsh. "I'm going to make you cum, too."

"I want you to cum, but later, not right now, we have to go talk to your dad and my mom and this is me teasing you. I'm invoking rule number nineteen."

She says this all fast as fuck and she's trying not to laugh or giggle or whatever and also I'm pretty fucking sure she's trying not to have an orgasm, too. I'm not positive on that last one, I'm just pretty fucking sure. I know an orgasm when I feel it, alright? I just know.

Also, fuck rule number nineteen. Who the fuck came up with rule number nineteen? Rule number nineteen can go eat a bag of dicks because I am pissed off right now.

I'm deep inside her, and I stare at her. Just staring. Not even blinking. This is a staring competition.

She's staring back at me, but she's cheating and blinking and also she's biting her bottom lip. Then she looks away from me and a red blush creeps up her cheek.

Fuck.

Seriously. Fuck.

"Are you serious?" I ask her.

She nods fast, refusing to look at me. "Uh huh."

"Are you sure you're serious?" I ask again. "I'll let you change your mind, Princess."

She doesn't answer me. Instead, she opens her mouth wide and shouts out, "Mom, can we make that bacon for breakfast?"

"Oh, they're awake!" Ashley's mom says, outside. "You want bacon, honey? What else? How about eggs and oatmeal? Is Ethan awake, too?"

"Wow," I say to the girl my cock is currently buried inside. "I've been betrayed."

I shake my head side to side, slow. She laughs and kisses me fast on the cheek.

"I love you, though," she says. Then louder, to her mom, she shouts, "Yup, Ethan's awake!"

"What's he doing?" my stepmom asks. "Does he want bacon and eggs and oatmeal?"

"You realize they're in the same tent?" my dad says. "If he's awake, he can hear you, too."

"Oh, that's true, huh?" my stepmom says. "Ethan! What are you doing? Do you want bacon and eggs and oatmeal?"

"Should I tell her what I'm doing right now?" I ask Ashley, sliding out of her a little before slamming back in. I grin and she stares at me, wide-eyed.

"Don't you dare!" she hisses at me. "You need to follow the rules, Ethan! Rule number nineteen. If we don't follow the rules, what's the point of even having them? I let you make up a rule just now, too. You have to let me tease you once. It's part of the rules."

Oh yeah? Well, two can play at that game. I pick up speed a little, going in for the kill. You think I don't know what you like, Princess? Nah... I may not be smart like you when it comes to college classes, but I've been paying attention when it comes to Ashley's Anatomy lessons.

"Yeah," I shout out, mostly to hide the sound of me thrusting into my perfect as fuck princess. "Bacon and eggs and oatmeal sounds great."

"Alright," my stepmom says. "You two come out here soon and we'll have breakfast and talk."

Mhm... yeah, we'll do that. Just give me a second.

I slide my hands under Little Miss Perfect Cocktease's ass and lift up her hips so I can move in just the right way and hit just the right spots. Oh, you thought I didn't know about that, Princess? Nah...

Her mouth opens wide in the shape of an "O" and her eyes clench shut. I can feel the start of her orgasm begging and pleading with my cock. As soon as she's just about to go over the edge, I pull out but I don't thrust back in. I leave her like that, laying in our shared sleeping bag, her mouth open, eyes shut, body taut and tight.

"Rule number nineteen," I tell her.

Her eyes snap open and she glares at me with wicked intent like she's got crazy witch powers or something. Holy fuck, she's seriously scary right now. Then her hand flies to her clit and it's pretty fucking obvious she's trying to finish what I started.

Oh, hell no! What's the point of rule number nineteen if I can't tease you, Princess? I grab her wrist and pull her hand away and we struggle like that. She kicks me. Seriously, she just kicked me. It's not like it hurt, but that's not the point.

Actually it's kind of funny and I start to laugh. This isn't good. I'm not supposed to be laughing. We're both basically naked and if anyone opens the tent, uh...

I smile at her, because I just want to fucking smile at her. She's beautiful and amazing and she's mine and maybe she's kind of mad right now, but it's not really mad. It's a playful mad. I'll give you plenty of orgasms later, Princess, don't worry.

I kiss her, and I mean it. There's a difference there, a difference between just kissing, or kissing because of lust, or a sweet and nice kiss, or kissing someone because you really fucking mean it. All sorts of different kinds of kissing, and this is the most important one.

She melts as soon as my lips touch hers, and she kisses me back. I let go of her hand and she reaches up and cups my cheeks in her palms. I hold her face, too, just wanting to kiss her and look at her. We stare into each other's eyes and there's a serious fucking spark going on or something. Her eyes glimmer and I'm pretty sure mine do, too, and our glimmer, that spark inside our souls, just reaches out and connects us together.

It's crazy. This entire thing is crazy. I love it. I love her.

"I love you," she says. "Even when you're an asshole like you just were.

I laugh. "I love you, too, Princess," I say. "Now let's get dressed and go eat breakfast and talk. Then we can sneak away to take a shower together so I can fuck your brains out."

"I need my brains," she says, making a cute pouty face at me. "I have a college scholarship to maintain, remember?"

"I mean, I guess we can put them back after?" I offer.

"Fuck my brains out and then... fuck me again to get them back in?"

Aw yeah. See, that's why Ashley's the smart one. She's got the best ideas, doesn't she? Seriously, that's some impressive intellect right there. I'm impressed.

Mia Clark

2 - Ashley

I WISH ETHAN HADN'T STOPPED me from having an orgasm. That's the only thing I can think about right now. We hurried and got dressed and everything seemed fine, but... nope, it's not.

I step out of the tent and everything is just sensitive. I can feel my panties rubbing against my clit, feel the gentle pressure of my shorts tight against my pussy, and I just kind of want to step back in the tent and zip myself in and um... do things that good girls don't do.

Do good girls do those things? Actually, I'm sure they probably do. I mean, I've done it before, but I was cautious and tactful, you know? I didn't exactly announce to the world what I was about to do, but right now I sort of don't care if the world knows because I just want to have an orgasm.

I was so close! So very very close, and just a couple of seconds more would have pushed me over the edge, but Ethan is a huge jerk.

I think I hate him. I don't actually hate him. I like him a lot, and I do love him, but I just don't like him right now.

When we step out of the tent, I give him a dirty look and stomp away, going to join my mom and Ethan's dad. They're sitting around the campfire already, toasting some bread. My mom offers me a piece that's already done and I take it and sit down across from her. Ethan wanders up, too, and my mom offers him a piece of toast, also.

I glare at him, but he just sits down next to me as if nothing's wrong.

I guess I can't blame him. I stopped him from having an orgasm, too. That was kind of fun, actually. I grin a little, remembering the intense look on his face, and then the shock and awe after I told him we needed to stop.

One thing I need to remember from all of this is that rule number nineteen is very dangerous. Actually, I think it may be the most dangerous rule of them all. The other rules are good, and should be used for good. Rule number nineteen can be used for evil purposes, but it can be used by both of us, so...

Except we've both used up our one tease for now, so the next time is going to be the real thing, and I'm really really excited! I guess rule number nineteen isn't all bad. It lets us spice things up a little.

My mother gives me a weird look and I belatedly realize I have a silly grin on my face and I probably look crazy.

"What's got you so happy this morning?" my mom asks.

"Um... it's just so nice to be awake!" I say, trying to sound chipper and enthusiastic.

Everyone gives me a weird look after that, including Ethan. *Ethan!* You're supposed to be on my side here! I stick my tongue out at him and scrunch up my nose. He gives me a dirty look, but then he smiles. I like the way he looks at me, with his eyes glimmering. It almost feels like he's looking straight into me, past everything, seeing all of my thoughts and feelings, but in a good way because I want him to see all of that and I want him to know it.

Sometimes it's hard to say stuff like that, though. It's easier if you don't have to say it, and it's easiest if you have someone who knows it without you having to say it. I guess I never thought about it before, but that's how it is with Ethan almost always. He makes me happy.

"I'm sure we're all glad to be awake," Ethan's dad says, laughing and shaking his head side to side. "I think, if no one minds, maybe we can just cut straight to the important topic that I'm sure we've all been waiting to talk about."

"And what's that, honey?" my mom asks him.

"The dating dilemma?" my stepdad says.

"It's not really a dilemma, though, is it?" she asks.

"I feel like I'm out of the loop here," he says. "I don't know who knows what or what's going on, so maybe we should start there?"

It makes sense. You start from the beginning, right? Except I'm not sure where the beginning started and by the looks of it, neither does anyone else. We sit around the campfire nibbling our toast and staring at each other.

"Alright!" my mom says, standing up, excited. "I've got an idea, everyone."

She hurries over to Ethan and has him stand, too. Then she moves his chair closer to mine.

"Sit, sit," she says, pushing him back to his seat. "And get really close to Ashley. Show us you're a couple. Make us believe it."

Ethan lifts one eyebrow and gives my mom a strange look, but he sits and cuddles close to me, wrapping his arm around my shoulder. I move into his touch, liking the fact that we can sit in front of our parents like this without worrying anymore.

I hope we don't have to worry, at least.

My mom goes back to her chair and scoots it closer to Ethan's dad. Then she sits and cuddles close to him, too.

"We're going to pretend we've just met and we don't know each other," my mom says. "All of us."

Um...

I glance at Ethan, and he looks at me. "Who are you?" I ask him.

"The man of your dreams, Princess," Ethan says.

"Ethan, you're supposed to pretend you don't know me. That's what my mom just said!"

"Listen, I'd say that to you if I didn't know you. I'd put my arm around you like this, too. You're the one screwing this up right here. How'd you know my name was Ethan, huh?"

"Shut up, you," I tell him, but everything he just said might be true. Ugh. *Ugh!*

"Um... alright, I meant that you two are still a couple and you know each other," my mom says. "I know Ethan's father, too. We're a couple. But we, meaning us parents over here, don't know you two over there. Pretend you aren't our children and we've just met you out and about while we're camping, and we invited you over for breakfast. That's what I meant."

"Oh," I say.

"Got it," Ethan says.

"What's the point of this?" my stepdad asks.

My mom ignores him and smiles at us. "Oh, you two look so cute! How long have you been together?"

"A little over a week," I say, smiling. "What about you two?"

"What is it, almost four years now?" my mom asks Ethan's dad.

"Just about," he says. "Our anniversary is soon."

"It is!"

"So... you said a little over a week? You two look awfully close for that short a time period," Ethan's dad says, staring pointedly at us. He smiles, too, but it's obvious what he's asking.

I decide to defer to Ethan with this one.

"Yeah, I guess so," Ethan says, shrugging.

I don't know why I deferred to Ethan with that one. He has failed me.

"I don't mean to pry," his dad says. "You hear a lot about summer love and relationships, falling hard and fast but it doesn't last for long, and I guess I should admit I'm a little curious."

"Honey..." my mom says to him, sighing.

"Nah, I get it," Ethan says. "Yeah, and you're totally right, too. I've seen that happen a lot before. I've known Ashley since the second grade. I guess we were seven or eight back then. I don't even remember anymore, but yeah, we've known each other for a long time. It might seem like it's a short amount of time for us to be dating, but we've got over ten years of history, so I think that counts for a lot."

I nod fast. "We used to play on the swings together at recess," I add. "Ethan was kind of a trouble maker, though."

"Awww, isn't that sweet?" my mom asks no one in particular. "I think it's sweet. It's very cute, you two!"

"Is that true?" my stepdad asks, giving us a curious look. "I knew you two knew each other before, but I didn't know you'd known each other that long. I didn't know about the recess thing."

"You must be thinking of someone else!" my mom interrupts. "We've just met Ethan and Ashley, remember?"

"Ohhh, right," my stepdad says, grinning. "Whoops. You look so much like my son, who is also named Ethan. Come to think of it, Ashley looks like my stepdaughter, too."

"It's a strange coincidence, I assure you!" my mom says, trying to pull us back on track.

"What are they like?" I ask. "Your son and stepdaughter, I mean."

"Hm..." Ethan's dad pauses to consider it. "Ashley's nice. She always gets good grades and she's polite and kind. Ethan... I'm not sure. I don't think he's a bad person, but I think we've had some struggles. I think I could have done a little better raising him as he was growing up, but I think he's going to be alright."

"Yeah, well, I've had some issues with my dad, too," Ethan says. "I know how it is, and maybe your son still wants you to be there for him. I wouldn't say that just because he's grown up now that he doesn't need you or anything."

"You think so?"

Ethan shrugs. "I don't know. Maybe you should have that conversation with him and ask him."

Ethan's dad smiles, considerate. "Maybe I will."

"Maybe Ashley could help, too?" I offer. "If she's polite and kind and gets good grades and Ethan is a little rough around the edges and struggling, and they're together now because, um... you're both married and they probably see each other a lot, er..."

"You know, I never really thought about that before. What do you think, honey?" my mom asks my stepdad.

"I don't know. They fight a lot," Ethan's dad says. "You think it'll work?"

"Alright, let's just get right to it," Ethan says. "Your son, your stepdaughter, what would you do if they started dating? Like, some serious shit, alright? Not just little stuff like hanging out, but intense like he gets an erection just thinking about her. Kind of fucked up, right? They probably have bedrooms right down the hall from each other. You want them sneaking around like that, because they're going to do it whether you want them to or not, or would you accept it and understand?"

Ethan's dad starts to choke and splutter. I stare at Ethan, mouth open, eyes wide, my entire face turning white. *Really, Ethan? Did you seriously just say that?*

My mom just starts to laugh maniacally, though. She seems really amused by all of this, and I think the rest of us are mortified, except for Ethan who is just kind of hanging out and laughing at my mom laughing.

Ugh.

I don't even know anymore.

After a couple of minutes everything calms down a little, and I guess we're, um... we're going to figure this out? I'm not sure.

"My son has a propensity towards seducing girls," Ethan's dad says. "I guess I hadn't thought about it before, but he very well might seduce his stepsister without me knowing it."

"I think they'd be cute together," my mom adds. "I don't think it would be seduction, per se, but I just think they'd be cute together. I think it'd work."

"I think it might work," my stepdad says. "I just have a problem believing it would."

"What the fuck, why?" Ethan asks, aggressive.

"Now, hold on! Let me explain this first."

Ethan grumbles and settles back into his chair. I reach for his hand and squeeze it tight, smiling at him.

"If he's going to sneak around, then I feel like it's something he's not proud of. It feels like it'd be something he's hiding, right?" his dad says. "If that's the case, then I don't know if I could accept that. I love my son, but Ashley's a part of the family now, too, and I love her and her mother, also."

"So you're saying that if he was open about it and talked to you about it, you'd be alright with it?" I ask.

"I think I could come to terms with it," my stepdad says. "It's difficult, because I've never thought of the two of them ever being in that situation. I'd prefer if they were considerate and didn't openly flaunt the fact that they were having sex together, even though I know they would be. I was a young man at one point, and even now me and my wife here like to have our share of sexy fun."

"Ewwww..."

"It's true, dear," my mom says to me. "We do like to have sexy fun. While you and Ethan were away at college... woo boy..."

"Mom! Seriously?"

"What! I wasn't the one having sex in a tent this morning."

Oh my God, they heard us? "...I don't know what you're talking about," I say, murmuring.

"Oh, right, sure you don't. If you think I believe that, you're quite mistaken, missy!"

"You're weird," I tell her. "You're just weird."

"It's genetic," she says, sticking her tongue out at me. "You're weird, too."

Ethan clears his throat, loud, and then stands up. He looks at me, then my mom, and finally to his dad.

"Look, I... I don't want to hide shit from you, alright? It wasn't about that. It wasn't that I was ashamed or thought I was doing anything wrong, but I didn't think you'd understand and I wanted to be with Ashley. I want to keep being with her, and whenever I thought about telling you and then thought about you getting pissed off about it, uh...

well, yeah, that's it. How am I supposed to date her if you're just pissed as fuck about us dating? That's why I didn't tell you, but I told her mom. I asked her if I could date Ashley, so I wasn't trying to hide it from anyone."

"He did ask me," my mom says. "He called me when we were on our trip. It was very polite and nice. I was so proud of him for doing that."

"You really did that?" his dad asks, smiling.

"Yeah," Ethan says.

He sits back down with me and I wrap my arms around him and hug him. He hugs me back and kisses me quick. Um... just quick, because our parents are right there, but I kind of want it to *not* be quick.

This is a bad thing to say, but to be honest I'm still kind of horny, and Ethan being so responsible and adamant about dating me is sexy and arousing in a way I didn't think was possible. I don't know if this is because of the teasing before or what. I think it's sexy either way.

Ugh, I'm a sex freak, aren't I? This is bad.

"I don't know why you didn't tell me earlier," his dad says. "When we came back from our trip and saw you and Ashley in the pool room, why didn't you just say something then? You two were cleaning and you acted like it was the same old same old. I guess I don't understand."

Oh... um... I start to blush. Also I remember what we were doing then. That was a really nice vibrator. Thinking about vibrators right now is probably the worst thing I can do.

Ethan's blushing, too, which isn't good. We're both quiet.

"Since no one's going to explain it, I will," my mom says. "They were having sex. On the pool table, too! With sex toys. I told them to do that in the privacy of their own room. It's not like we have sex on the pool table, so they shouldn't, either."

Surprisingly, um... Ethan's dad says, "We did a few times while they were away, didn't we?"

My mom stares at him, her mouth open. "You can't tell them that! Not after I yelled at them for doing it!"

"It's my pool table. I paid for it. I think I can use it however I want."

"Ewww," I say. "Really? Eww!"

"That's just fucking gross," Ethan says, shaking his head. "Good job, though, Dad. High five."

And they do. Ethan and his dad give each other a high five.

"Ethan, you can't high five your dad for having sex with my mom. That's super weird!"

"What? They're married. Obviously they're having sex."

"On the pool table!"

Ethan shrugs. His dad shrugs, too. I glare at the both of them.

"We cleaned it off after, Ashley," my mom says. "You don't have to worry about that. There's no cross-contamination or anything."

"Mom," I say, staring at her, unblinking.

"I'm just saying, honey," she says.

"I thought we were all pretending we didn't know each other? What ever happened to that?"

"Yeah, that was kind of fun," my stepdad says, then to my mom he adds, "It was interesting. I'm glad you thought of that, hun."

"Yeah, it was cool," Ethan says. "But, uh... seriously, though. Real talk here for a second. I know that Ashley is your stepdaughter and so I guess that makes her like a daughter to you, so I'm just going to ask you, too, like I asked her mom. Uh..."

All eyes are on Ethan. I watch him carefully. This is new and different, and...

"Sir..." Ethan says, struggling with the word. "I'd like to date your daughter."

"No way," my stepdad says immediately. "Not happening."

"What! You can't say that," my mom says. "That was so nice and sweet, Ethan. Don't listen to your father. I'll let you date Ashley as long as you want, but only if as long as you want is forever."

"Mom, *really?*" I say. "You're going to scare him. You're scaring me, even. That's just creepy sounding."

"It's not creepy, it's the truth."

Ethan's dad stands up and goes over to Ethan. Ethan stands, too, but looks a little confused. His dad holds out his hand and Ethan takes it. They shake hands for a second, but then my stepdad puts his other hand around his son and pulls him in for a hug.

"I was just kidding," Ethan's dad says. "I've always wanted to say that, though. It's one of those things. If you have a daughter some day, you'll understand."

"Wow," Ethan says, grunting. "Really, Dad? Wow."

"I'm fine with you and Ashley dating. Just be careful with each other, alright? You both mean a lot to me and it would kill me if either one of you got hurt."

"Yeah, I know," Ethan says.

I look up at them and smile. Ethan's dad smiles down at me, too.

"The opposite is true, too, though," he says. "It would make me extremely happy to see the both of you happy, and if you're happy together, then so be it."

"Awww," my mom says, gushing. "Ashley, isn't that sweet?"

I smile, because it is. It's nice. I feel like we've accomplished a lot today, and the day just started, so it's like we've accomplished even more.

"I don't want to find out about you having sex on the pool table again, though," my stepdad says.

He points right at me, too. *Oh no.*

"You better not corrupt my son, young lady," Ethan's dad says to me.

"What! Me?"

"You don't even know the half of it," Ethan says. "Seriously, this girl's a freak."

"Ashley, really?" my mom asks. "Are you a freak?"

"Mom! I am not."

"If you want to talk about it later, I'm here for you, honey," she says. "If you have any questions at all, I'll try to answer them as best I can."

"Mom... please stop?"

Really. Really really. This is weird.

It's kind of nice, too. Nice in an embarrassing way, but still nice. I'm glad we can all still be, um... I guess it's a family? A weird family, maybe. Ethan's not really my family. He's my stepbrother, yes, but he's my boyfriend now and I don't know if he can be both.

Stepbrother boyfriend with benefits?

He winks at me and comes back to sit down next to me while his dad goes back over to my mom, too. My mom and his dad start figuring out the rest of our breakfast, apparently starting with eggs.

Ethan leans over and whispers into my ear. "Hope you're ready, Princess. Now that that's all settled, once we're done with breakfast I'm going to drag you to the showers. No more teasing, this time is for real..."

Oh no... I'm in trouble, aren't I?

Very very good trouble...

3 - Ethan

BREAKFAST IS NICE. If I'm being completely fucking honest, breakfast is always nice, though. Who doesn't like breakfast? For real, that's just weird as fuck. I get not having time for breakfast, or maybe not feeling hungry in the morning sometimes, but other than that, breakfast is amazing.

Everything else is pretty great so far, too. My dad and I talk over food and Ashley and her mom talk, too. We all just talk together, one big happy family or whatever the fuck you want to call it. I guess it's kind of weird if you think about it as me and my dad and my stepmom and stepsister, but it doesn't have to be like that.

I mean, really, how is this any different from just hanging out with my girlfriend and her mom, and then my dad is there, too? It's like in-laws or something. One in-law.

Fuck, what happens if that happens? What do I call Ashley's mom then? Mom, I guess. Actually, yeah, that works, but how do I refer to her to others? Do I say she's my stepmom or my mother-in-law or what?

Fuck.

I think I have some time before I have to worry about that, though. Calm the fuck down, Ethan! It's only been about a week. That's way too soon for marriage and babies and all of that. Holy fuck, where'd babies come from?

So, hey, how about that breakfast? Good, right? Yeah...

We finish up eating and I help my dad put the fire out and clear everything away. Ashley and her mom are cleaning up what they can. We're going to have to bring these pans up front to clean them off later, but we've got time.

There's no real rush or anything. That's one of the things I like about camping, especially without phones or whatever the fuck else. You just kind of live in the moment and you don't worry about everything else. Do you know how liberating it is to not even know what time it is and to have no real reason to care? Yeah, we can just turn the car on and check the radio to figure it out, but right now it doesn't matter and it might not even matter for a week or two.

We can just have fun. My dad knows about my relationship with Ashley, and he's cool with it. Ashley's mom knows. Even Caleb knows, which I guess is good? Fuck if I know. It's good because now he won't try to put the moves on Ashley and if he does I have an excuse to kick his ass. Don't even make me do it, campground boy.

"Hey," I say, because, yeah, I'm just going to live in the moment right now. "I'm going to go take a shower."

"Alright," my dad says. "Sounds nice. I'll probably head over there in a few, too. Just want to take care of some things here."

"If you find a hair dryer, let me know!" my stepmom says.

Ashley just kind of fidgets around, nervous. I sneak over and give her a quick kiss before heading to our tent to grab my stuff. As soon as I come out, something happens, though. It's kind of crazy, actually.

"Um... I think I'm going to go take a shower, too..." Ashley says, kind of shy and cute as fuck.

"Are you now?" her mom asks, grinning wide.

"Should just take a shower with Ethan," my dad says, grinning, too. "Save some quarters."

"That's not why I'm going!" she shouts, almost squeaking a little.

It's kind of funny and I start to laugh. My dad and her mom tease her a little more, but she ignores them and stomps over to the tent to grab her things, too. I wait for her, because I'm a nice guy like that. Yeah, high quality boyfriend material right here, don't you forget it.

Ashley comes out of the tent, and when she sees me waiting for her, she looks a little surprised.

"What's that look for?" I ask her, smirking.

"Were you waiting for me?" she asks.

"Yeah?"

"Oh."

"Oh?"

"Go!" my stepmom says. "Go take a shower. Hurry up so we can plan our day!"

"Hey, listen," I counter, trying to put on a straight face. "I have to make sure I clean up nice. Need to be presentable. Respectability takes time, alright?"

"Oh, right," Ashley says, rolling her eyes at me. "Who are you trying to impress, Ethan?"

"You, for starters," I tell her.

She starts to blush. My stepmom gives me a silent nod and a thumbs up behind Ashley's back. My dad just sighs and shakes his head.

"Come on, Princess," I say, nudging her elbow with mine. "Let's go shower. I don't know what these freaks over here think we're going to be doing, but all I'm planning on doing is showering."

"Oh, um... yup!" Ashley says, nodding fast. "That's all we're going to be doing is showering."

"You're blowing our cover," I tell her.

"What do you mean I'm blowing our cover? We're just going to shower, Ethan."

"Listen, literally no one is going to buy that the way you're saying it."

"How am I even saying it? I'm not saying it any weird way. You're dumb."

"It's true," her mom says. "We're not buying it, honey."

"Not at all," my dad says.

"You don't have to buy anything!" Ashley says in protest. "I'm... I'm going to take a shower with my boyfriend and that's all!"

Oooooh damn. She played the *boyfriend* card. This just got real.

Yeah, well, seriously, though. Shower. We don't have all day here, Princess. I start to head over there, walking slow. She doesn't notice at first.

"It looks like your boyfriend is leaving you behind, though," her mom tells her.

"What?" Ashley spins around and sees me walking away. It's not even that far, maybe ten feet or something, but she stares at me wide-eyed like I've traveled across the country without telling her. "Ethan! Where are you going?"

"Uh, showers? They're up front?"

She puts her hands on her hips and glares at me, which is pretty entertaining considering her hands are filled with a small tote bag of shower essentials and her change of clothes.

"Ugh!" she says.

Ugh? Yeah, sure, let's go with it. If the worst thing that happens to me today is a silly, pouty "ugh" from Ashley, then today's going to be fucking perfect.

Mia Clark

4 - Ashley

I'M JUST GOING TO TAKE A SHOWER. I am *just* going to take a shower. I *am* just going to take a shower.

I repeat this mantra over and over again. I don't know who I'm trying to convince, because it's just Ethan and I walking right now, but I feel like I should be ready just in case, right? What if someone sees us and they ask where we're going.

"I'm just going to take a shower!" I say out loud. This is practice.

"Who are you even talking to?" Ethan asks, giving me a weird look, one eye-brow raised.

"Um..."

From out of the woods behind us, a giant furry animal comes running over. It's the dog.

"I'm talking to the dog!" I tell Ethan. "I didn't want him to worry about where we were going."

"Look, Princess. Talking to the dog is my thing," Ethan says. "You can't talk to the dog like that."

The dog comes trotting up beside us, walking with us, his tongue sticking out, panting happily.

"I can talk to the dog however I want," I say. Turning to the dog, I add, "Right? You like when I talk to you, don't you, Gilgamesh?"

"Did you just call the dog Gilgamesh? Are you trying to name my dog right out from under me?"

"He's not your dog, Ethan," I say, sticking out my tongue at him. "You found him in the woods, but he's not yours."

"No way, of course he is," Ethan says. "We're best buds. Right, Dog?"

"You can't just call him Dog. He needs a real name."

"Oh, yeah? Like Gilgamesh? What's that even mean?"

"He was a Sumerian King!" I say. "I watched this anime once and in it Gilgamesh was the King of All Heroes and Possessor of Everything, too. It was really interesting, actually. I don't think that's historically accurate, but I liked the idea a lot."

"Wait, what are you doing watching anime?" Ethan asks.

"Um... what do you mean? I was just watching it... no reason..."

Is that too nerdy? Oh my God, it's too nerdy, isn't it? I didn't think about this. I bet Ethan thinks I'm weird now. Weird in a bad way, I mean.

I don't think it is, though. I thought the show was interesting, and I still do! I would watch it again, even. I...

"Look, did you like it or not? Don't go doing that wishy-washy bullshit thing where you try to pretend you're not into it just to impress me. How does that even work? I don't get it."

"Um... I did like it. Yes?"

This is when he breaks up with me, isn't it? Well, I have news for you, Ethan. You can't break up with me. It's one of the rules. Rule number twenty.

"That's cool," Ethan says. "What was it called? I used to watch anime a lot when I was younger, but I haven't had a chance to do it for awhile now."

"Wait, what? You? Ethan Colton, star quarterback of the football team, muscle-bound jock, bad boy extraordinaire--"

He interrupts me with a narrow-eyed, furrowed brow look, his nose scrunched up and his lips curled and everything.

"Where do you think I learned how to be such a badass?" Ethan asks, sounding proud of himself.

I just laugh. "I don't believe you. You're lying."

"Hey, I wouldn't lie to you. I think that's one of our rules, isn't it?"

"Um... yup. Sort of. Rule number seven," I tell him.

"I've watched a few," he says. "It's the voices, though. They sound weird sometimes."

"That's why you watch it with subtitles," I say with a nod. "Then you get the original tone and inflection of the Japanese voice actors, but you can read the subtitles in English and know what they're saying. I guess you could learn Japanese, too. I'd like to some day, but it's not a high priority. Once I'm done my core classes in college I was thinking about..."

"Whoa whoa whoa," Ethan says, grinning.

The dog barks at me, too. Wait, he's not just the dog! Gilgamesh, King of Heroes!

He helped bring Ethan back to me, and so I think he's deserving of that title. Because I kind of think maybe Ethan is my hero, so, um...

"Who knew that Little Miss Perfect had a secret life as some crazy anime princess? Crazy, man..."

"I am not!" I say.

Gilgamesh barks at Ethan, too.

"See, he agrees with me?"

"We should watch that show," Ethan says. "With the subtitles or whatever. When we get back from camping. It sounds pretty cool."

"What, really?" I say, confused.

Ethan intentionally bumps into me while we're walking. "Yeah, really. Why not?"

"With Gilgamesh, too?" I ask.

"Maybe he needs a nickname or something," Ethan says, contemplative. "How about Hero?"

"Ooh, that's a nice name. I like it."

"Hero?" Ethan says to the dog formerly known as Gilgamesh. Hero barks in approval.

"I think he likes you," I say.

We're almost to the front now, almost to the showers. And... we have a dog with us. Um... how am I supposed to seduce my stepbrother in the shower when there's a dog with us? I mean, obviously Hero won't be in the shower with us, but we can't exactly keep him out, either. There's space under the stall doors and he could sneak in, and...

Caleb spots us through the window in the front office. A second later he comes out, jogging towards us. He waves, then notices the dog with us. Hero barks a greeting to Caleb, and Caleb goes over to pat him, scruffing up his neck.

"Hey, uh... hey," Caleb says, nervous.

"Hey," Ethan says, cool and relaxed.

He's not fooling anyone, though! Or, I guess he's fooling everyone but me. Ethan is being slightly nicer to Caleb today, which I think is good. We need to help Caleb later, so it better be good, at least.

"Hi, Caleb!" I say, trying to show the enthusiasm that Ethan's lacking. "How are you?"

"Good," Caleb says, smiling while he pets Hero. "I told my dad everything that happened. Uh... not everything. The short version, I guess? Anyways, he's looking into it, but he thinks the dog might be an old stray. He could have been out there for awhile, but he seems alright. My dad's going to look into it a little, but he thinks he might have belonged to this guy who lived nearby awhile ago. He moved, though, so..."

"So?" Ethan says, defensive.

"We can bring him to the local humane society for you," Caleb says. "My dad doesn't mind. They can check him for fleas and get him updated on his shots and all of that. He looks fine, but you never know. A dog like him should do good around here, too. Someone will adopt him."

"Wait, hold up," Ethan says. "You're not taking Gilgamesh."

"Oh, he's Gilgamesh now?" I ask, giggling. "I thought you didn't like that name?"

"His full name. He needs to sound like a real badass. Gilgamesh Colton, King of Heroes, for real."

"Er...?" Caleb scrunches up his brow and gives Ethan a strange look.

"Colton-Banks," I add. "That's his last name, I think."

"Yeah," Ethan says. "Yeah, that sounds good. Makes it more legit."

"I don't understand what you're saying," Caleb says. "Who's Gilgamesh... Colton-Banks?"

"The dog," Ethan says, jerking his head towards the dog. "Seriously, weren't you listening, kid? You can't adopt away my dog. I'm keeping him."

"You're just going to keep some dog you found in the woods?" Caleb asks. "I don't think that's how this works."

"Why the fuck not?" Ethan asks.

"Er... I don't know?"

"It's the same as someone else adopting him, isn't it?" I ask.

"Yeah... I guess..."

"But, hey, do you mind dogsitting for us for a second?" Ethan says, quick. "We're going to go take a shower."

Oh! Oh oh oh, I planned for this! I practiced and everything!

"We're *just* going to take a shower!" I say, steady and firm.

Ethan, Caleb, and Hero look at me like I have two heads. What? What did I do?

"You're fucking weird, Princess," Ethan says, laughing. "Seriously."

"Are you two... in the shower..." Caleb says?

"Caleb! What did I just say!" *Really, I just said it!* "I said we're just going to take a shower! That's it!"

"No one's even buying that, Princess," Ethan says. "You don't have to pretend anymore."

"I'm not pretending," I say, pouting and glaring at Ethan.

"Oh, uh... I can watch the dog, though," Caleb says. "Does he know any tricks?"

"Yeah," Ethan says. "He knows every trick. All of them."

"Oh, cool," Caleb says. "Shake?" he asks Hero, holding out his hand.

Hero sits down and stares at Caleb's hand, his tongue lolling out of his mouth. After a second he nudges against Caleb's hand like he wants to be petted.

"He only listens to cool people," Ethan says. "You've got to up your game, kid."

"What? That's not true, is it?" Caleb asks. "Ashley, is that truc? I'm cool, right? Kind of... And we're the same age, Ethan! I'm not a kid. You're the same age as me."

"Don't worry, you'll grow up to be as cool as me one day, Caleb. I'll help you out, bro."

"We really appreciate you watching Hero for us, though," I say, smiling. "Um... you can call him that instead of Gilgamesh. I was just making up weird names for him. If our parents are alright with it, we can adopt him and take him home with us, too. I think bringing him to the vet or whatever you think needs to be done is good, though. Can you help us with that?"

This is serious. Caleb nods, determined. "Yes, I will help. He seems like a cool dog, too. I'll see if I can teach him how to shake while I'm watching him."

"I told you, he only listens to cool people," Ethan says, shrugging. "You don't have to worry about it."

"I'm cool!" Caleb says. "I'll show you. Hero will shake with me by the time you're done, um... just showering..."

"We're just going to take a shower, Caleb!" I shout.

Seriously, why does no one believe me?

Mia Clark

5 - *Ashley*

W E'RE JUST TAKING A SHOWER, Ethan," I say, kind of mumbling and nervous.

I really shouldn't be nervous. There's nothing to worry about anymore, right? We basically just walked into the shower stall without a care in the world, and while no one saw us, I'm not sure it would have mattered, either. It did seem a little sneaky, though, and I did peek both ways to make sure no one was watching us go into the shower together.

Because, really, it's not exactly strange to shower together, and Caleb said that people do it for any number of reasons besides sexy ones, but I'm not sure I believe him.

Also this isn't sexy. Nuh uh. Nope! This is just, um... we're just taking a shower.

"Oh yeah?" Ethan asks, staring at me with one eyebrow raised, a horribly mischievous look on his face. "You keep telling yourself that, Princess."

"I'm being serious!" I say, stomping one foot down and standing tall. Serious! That's what this is.

Ethan puts his things on the bench opposite the showerhead. There's plenty of room between the two, so everything should be fine, but it's just the way he does it. Just puts his clothes down on the bench, sets up his shampoo and conditioner and everything, then starts taking off his shirt like I'm not even there with him.

He does it slow, too, teasing the cloth up his torso, lifting it slowly so that I can see every inch of his body being revealed. He even tightens his abs, flexing for me while I watch him strip. When he's done, he tosses his shirt next to the rest of his clothes.

Then he looks at me. I... um...

I'm clinging to my clothes, holding them tight to my chest. I don't know what to do. I really don't know what to do. What are we supposed to be doing?

We've done this so many times before, and I think it should be so easy right now. It should be easy because our parents know, and there's no need to hide it, but...

What are we hiding? We're just taking a shower!

Ethan walks towards me, standing close. Very quietly, he takes my clothes from me and puts them on the bench next to his. I'm still holding my hands close to my chest, kind of guarded, but that doesn't bother him. He steps even closer to me, my hands tight between my chest and his bare chest now. He wraps his arms around me, holding me tight. His fingers dip beneath the bottom of my shirt, touching my bare skin.

I tremble at his touch, and I look up, my lip quivering, body shaking.

Ethan pulls me close to him, his hips pressing against mine. I still have my hands between us, but that's it. I don't know what to do with them, so I just leave them there while I look up at him. He smiles down at me, and then he kisses me on the nose.

"You just want to take a shower, Princess?" he asks.

I nod fast. It's not that I don't want to do more, it's just...

He wraps his fingers in the bottom of my shirt and lifts it up. My arms stop him, though.

"Lift up," he says, kissing me quick.

I do as he says, lifting my hands. Slow and careful, taking his time, Ethan pulls my shirt up and away, then tosses it with our clothes. He moves to unsnap my bra after, removing it with expert precision. I guess that's one of the benefits of dating a bad boy? He definitely doesn't have any trouble removing my bra.

I laugh a little, and Ethan smiles. He puts my bra with the rest of our clothes, and then we're standing there, front to front, our upper bodies completely naked.

"We're just taking a shower, right?" he says to me.

Yes, he says this, but his hand sneaks towards my stomach, his fingers trailing a smooth line up past my belly button, then further still until he's cupping the underside of my breast.

"J-just a sh-shower," I say, my teeth chattering.

I shiver and I try to pretend I'm cold, but mostly it's because he moves his thumb up until it rubs lightly at my nipple. The rest of his hand holds just under my breasts, his fingers pressing lightly at the sides.

"Mhm, just a shower," Ethan says, smiling and kissing me again. "We've got to take your shorts off, though."

My eyes grow wide and I look up at him again. "Um... alright..."

While he cups one of my breasts, his other hand moves towards the front of my shorts. He unzips them first, then undoes the button one handed. His hand slips beneath the waistband of my shorts in the front, then circles around towards the back, moving a little lower as he does, making my shorts fall slowly. When his hand is entirely behind me, he presses his fingers into the curves of my butt, squeezing slightly.

"Underwear off, too, Princess," Ethan says. "They've got to go. Do you want to do it, or do you want me to?"

I bury my face in his shoulder, nervous and aroused and embarrassed and...

"You," I murmur into his warm skin. "Please."

"Alright, babygirl," he says. "You're going to have to help me a little here."

He moves both hands down to my hips this time, dipping his fingers beneath the waistband of my panties. Slowly, he moves my underwear downwards, but he bends lower, too. He shifts away from me, my face no longer pressed against his shoulder, and kneels down. My panties follow suit until he's got them to my ankles. I lift one foot up, stepping out of them, then the other, and now I'm completely naked.

Deceptively soft and sweet, Ethan kisses the front of my thigh. His hands move behind my legs, his fingers wrapping around my soft skin, and ever so slightly he pulls my legs apart. His lips kiss across the inside of my thighs now, moving from one to the other, slowly working his way up.

I can feel his hot, heavy breath against the center of my body, tickling and teasing at my clit. His breathing grows heavier and I clench my eyes shut. Oh, yes, he's going to kiss me there, isn't he?

Um... nope...

He stands again, standing in front of me once more.

"Just a shower," he says with a nod, smiling.

"Um..."

I open my eyes and watch him, my bottom lip trembling so hard that I have to pull it into my mouth and clench it between my teeth to stop it from shaking.

Ethan unbuttons and unzips his shorts, letting them slide down his legs. He kicks them aside, then pulls down his underwear. We're both naked now. Both very very naked, and... um...

He reaches towards his change of clothes and grabs some of the quarters he brought with him. "Just give me a second," he says. "Be right back."

I watch him turn around and go to put the quarters in the shower so we can start. Just showering. That's what we're about to start. I think. Maybe. I don't even really know?

We're just taking a shower!

As soon as he turns around, I realize we're definitely not just taking a shower, though.

Ethan's cock is hard. It's maybe harder than I've ever seen it. Pointing straight at me and slightly up, it bobs with a certain sense of confidence and promise. I look down. I can't take my eyes off of him, away from his... erection... I...

Ethan walks towards me with purpose. He wraps his arms around me, his hands pressing tight against my ass, and then he lifts me up in one fluid motion. My legs wrap around his waist instinctively, and I grab at his shoulders and neck, too. I cling to him, holding tight.

Water cascades all around us as Ethan carries me towards the shower. I can feel his cock slapping lightly against me, throbbing and begging to slide its way inside my arousal-slick folds. Yes, um... I'm wet. Not just from the shower. I've been this way for awhile now, probably since this morning after our botched attempt at teasing each other into submission.

Ethan lowers me, lodging the head of his cock between the folds of my glistening sex. Just a little lower and we'll be together completely, he'll be filling me entirely.

He both growls and purrs into my ear, heady and strong, yet seductive and sweet, too.

"Tell me to stop, Princess," he says. "Tell me that we're just taking a shower and I'll put you down and stop. Otherwise, the rules are the rules. I can't tease you this time, Princess. It's going to be for real."

As if that isn't enough, he adds, "I want to fuck you so bad, Ashley. I want to feel you around my cock. Please, Princess? I promise I'll make it worth your while, babygirl."

I whimper and nod a little, pressing my face hard against his cheek. Ethan lowers me a little, and then a little more. I can feel him inside me, pressing his way further into me, inch by inch. It's so deliriously arousing and with every small movement further inside me, my pussy clenches and spasms. It's almost like my body is trying to grab at his cock and pull him all the rest of the way in.

"Halfway in, Princess," he says, moving forward to kiss the side of my neck. "You just say the word and I'll stop, alright? I don't want to tease you, though. I want to make love to you so fucking bad."

I don't say anything. I don't even try to say anything. I'm trying so hard not to say anything that my lips are pursed shut, tight, and I'm pretty sure they're turning white from how hard I'm keeping my mouth closed.

Ethan shifts his head back, watching me. I move back, too, staring into his eyes. Our noses are touching, tip to tip. He slides me down his cock a little more, tempting and provocative, and then he bucks his hips up while also pulling me down.

I can't keep my lips tight any longer. My mouth opens, wide, and I let out a lusty moan. The sound of my ecstasy echoes through the shower stall, accompanying the pitterpatter of water falling down on us and all around us. Ethan squeezes my ass hard and pulls me even harder onto his cock, filling me completely.

I feel him throb and pulse inside me and I can't stop myself from clenching against him. He grinds his hips against mine, the center of his body rubbing and stroking at my clit.

"Aw yeah," he says. "I want you to fucking scream for me, Princess."

"Ethan, I... w-we're in the shower," I tell him, but it doesn't seem to matter.

While holding me aloft, he lifts me up slightly and pulls his hips back. Then he thrusts forward and pulls me down again. Our bodies clap together, loud, and my mind goes blank for a second. Oh my God... oh my God...

"What's wrong?" Ethan asks, smirking, cocky. "We're just taking a shower, right?"

Holy... wow... yes, um...

I'm more worked up than I thought, or Ethan is better than I knew. Except I think both those things might be true. It seems like the more we're together, the better we know each other, and each time we have sex is so much better than the last. It seems almost crazy in a way. How can that even happen? You'd think it'd be the same, especially considering the same is certainly very good, but...

Nope. Not at all.

"I stopped before, remember?" he asks me. "Right when you were about to cum, Princess. I stopped right then. I know exactly how far I can go before you're about to orgasm. You know that, right?"

I nod and I kiss him and I dig my fingernails into his shoulders, clinging tight to him.

"I'm not going to tease you, Princess. Rules are rules, right? I'm going to tell it to you straight. You know as well as I do that I know what I'm doing. I think I can make you cum in... maybe fifteen or twenty more seconds. What do you think?"

I don't know how to think right now. Ooohhh, it feels so good. I nod, though. I'm sure he's right. I know a lot about math and science, history and literature, but this is Ethan's specialty. This is a subject he's intimately familiar with in more ways than one, and if they taught classes like this in college he'd most certainly get high marks. I doubt he'd even be taking a class like that, though. He'd be teaching it.

"Maybe ten seconds now. You can feel it building up, Princess. I know you can. Each thrust, the perfect rhythm, but here's the catch. I want more. I'm greedy as fuck and I want more. You've got five seconds, Princess. I don't care what you have to do. I want you to cum in five seconds, or we really are just going to take a shower, nothing else."

Um...? Wait, what! No. No no no. That's... that's not fair. I tell him as much, wide-eyed and frantic.

"Ethan, no, no, Ethan no no no, I want to, I want to cum please please please."

He grins at me and shakes his head. "Four seconds now, Princess." Another second passes and he says, "Three..."

I need to take drastic measures here. I cling tight to him, my upper body pressing hard against his. When he thrusts into me again, I grind the center of my body against him. Ohhh... oh my God, yesss...

I can feel it. Feel more. I don't know why I never thought of this before. My clit slides along Ethan's shower-slick stomach, a jolt of sharp pleasure crashing through me. He pulls out and slams back into me hard and I writhe against him.

"Two, Princess," he says. Then, soon after. "One..."

One. I have one. Can I do this? I think yes. He tries to pull out of me, and I don't know if it's because he's going to thrust back in or if this is it. I don't have more time. I need to. I need to cum and climax and orgasm and even though those are essentially the same exact thing, I need to do all three at once, together and separately. I...

I press my lips hard against his, kissing him in some vague hope of distraction, and then I bring my body to pleasure, feeling his cock throb deep inside of me while I slip and slide my clit across the rugged grooves of his lower abs.

"Oh my gosh oh my gosh, wow..." I say. That's sort of what I wanted to say, at least, but I think it just comes out as gibberish.

"That's it, Princess," he says. "Cum for me. I want to feel it. I want to..."

I keep pressing against him, bucking my hips against him, too. I stare hard into his eyes, feeling ecstasy overtake me, and then I see something amazing. Ethan looks surprised for a second, and then excited.

"Fuck, I'm--"

He doesn't have to say more. I can feel it. He's excited and I'm excited and now we're both cumming, our orgasms mutual and complete. My body throbs around him, clenching at his pulsing shaft, and he shoots stream after stream of sweet sticky cream deep inside me. Oh, I love it. I absolutely love it. I kiss him and hold him and I just keep writhing against him. Now that I know this is something I can do, that I'm allowed to do, I can't seem to stop.

My clit throbs and screams with pleasure, my entire body overloaded with orgasmic desire. I kiss Ethan's lips and his cheeks and his nose, his face, his eyes. All of him. I can't stop. He slaps my ass, hard and rough, then squeezes tight and drives his cock into me as deep as he can. I can feel him there, so very far inside me, cumming harder than I've ever felt him cum before, his seed splashing directly against...

Some weird thought overcomes me. What if I wasn't on birth control? I... I am... I think I am. Sometimes it doesn't work, though. Right? What if this is it? Or this is that? I mean, what if this is the time that it fails and if it did, um...

Warmth and desire fills me, and I think about us having a baby.

I tell him this, whispering into his ear while my climax smolders and simmers low. "What if I'm pregnant?" I ask him. "You're so far inside me, Ethan. What if I'm pregnant now?"

"Fuck, Princess... what are you..."

He just came inside me, but as soon as I ask him about pregnancy, he gets harder. His cock throbs and pulses, stretching. I squeeze back against him instinctively, and I feel a shimmer of pleasure working its way back to me. I wriggle and grind against him, pressing my clit against him again.

"Do you want me to have your baby?" I ask him. "What would you do? Would you still find me attractive if my belly was big and growing and..."

"Holy fucking shit, you're insane," he says, but his erection gives him away.

He's immediately hard, almost as if he never came inside me in the first place. His fingers squeeze tight into my ass and he starts to thrust again, driving deep into me.

"I want it," I say, begging and pleading with him. "I want you. I want to have a baby with you, Ethan. I... I forgot to take my birth control the first night we were here. I was so worried about you last night that I forgot to take it then, too. I can. I can get pregnant now. I want you to make me pregnant, Ethan. Please?"

"Fucking... are you serious?" he asks, staring at me, wide-eyed.

He keeps thrusting into me, though. He's slamming even harder inside me, harder than before.

I bite my bottom lip and look at him, shy. "Mmhmm..."

6 - Ethan

WHATEVER HAPPENS, it's your own damn fucking fault, Princess," I say to her. "There's no way I'm stopping now."

"Ethan, you..." She whimpers when I thrust hard into her, her body slamming hard against mine. "You can't, you..."

Fuck, she's good. She is so fucking good it hurts.

This is crazy, though. I literally have no idea what's going on. I have a strict "No Pregnancy" policy. I kind of already broke that before with her, though. Rule number whatever-the-fuck it was, the one I made up, where I specifically told her we weren't going to use condoms for the week because I knew she was on birth control.

Yeah, it's nice. It's a first for me, too. I don't fuck around. When I said there was a strict "No

Pregnancy" policy, I meant it. Yeah, alright, so girls before tried to convince me it was fine, that they were on birth control or whatever the fuck, but to be completely fucking honest, some women are crazy.

I'm not saying *most*, so just calm yourself, alright? Most women are fine, and I have a certain general affection for the female gender, but it doesn't matter if most women are fine, because it only takes one to fuck you up hard. This isn't the good kind of fucked up, either. This is the bad kind where you get a phone call in a year telling you that you're a father.

Nah, I don't need that kind of responsibility. I don't even fucking want it. I'm careful, or I was careful, and Ashley Fucking Banks screwed it all up.

It doesn't help that I don't even fucking care if she gets pregnant. It doesn't help that I really kind of fucking want her to get pregnant. The thought is so fucking intoxicating and arousing that my cock is the hardest I can ever remember it being. This is my erection's entire life's purpose and it is ready and willing to do its duty.

I don't know if I'd be a good dad. To be honest, I'd probably be a bad one. I trust Ashley to tell me I'm being a dumb fuck and to be better, though. I trust that she'd help me figure this shit out and become the most awesome fucking dad ever.

But... yeah... hold the fuck up, alright?

I'm still pretty sure I don't want to get her pregnant right now. That's what I'm telling myself, but then why is my cock hard as fuck, why do I keep slamming hard into her, fucking her with reckless abandon, all while she whimpers and whispers about how I can't do this, how she's going to get pregnant, how...

Oh, fuck. Fuck, fuck fuck...

"I'm cumming, Ethan, I'm cumming," she gasps, moaning into my ear. "Don't cum now, alright? Wait until I'm done. The easiest time for a girl to get pregnant is when she's having an orgasm because it helps assist the man's cum in getting closer to her womb, so you... you can't... not now... just... just wait..."

This is like some serious informational and educational shit right here. Is it true? Fuck if I know. All I know is it makes me even harder, makes me even more aroused knowing that if I cum right now when she's having her orgasm that...

Yeah, well, guess what the fuck happens? It's kind of obvious, isn't it? It feels amazing as fuck, too.

I fill her the fuck up. For good measure, I hold her down hard on my cock, too. There's no fucking way she could even hope to get away. She's squirming and begging and pleading with me, whispering, "No, no no noooo," into my ear all while her greedy fucking pussy squeezes and clenches and begs me for more. Yes, yes, yesss...

I don't know what happens after that. I think I black out or something. Crazy, right? Yeah, uh... I don't even know.

I close my eyes and when I open them again, we're sitting under the hot water of the shower. Princess fucking Ashley is still impaled on my cock, which is pretty great. I'm sitting on a bench on this side, right beneath the showerhead, and she's just sitting in my lap. No more sex. I don't even think I can get hard right now.

I mean, yeah, I think I could probably get hard. It's hard not to get hard with Ashley trying to seduce the fuck out of me. I think we're both tired, though.

I thought showers were supposed to be nice and refreshing? Why am I exhausted as fuck, then? Seriously, what the fuck?

She rains kisses all over my face while the shower rains on each of us. A little more time passes, and eventually the water turns off. We're left in some sense of serenity, the gentle drip drip drip of whatever water is left slowly dropping down onto us.

Yeah, uh... now that we're done, now that I have some time to think, I have a few choice things to say to this girl.

The first is, "Holy fuck."

She grins at me, unable to contain herself. She looks super fucking happy with herself, and smug, too. Yeah, you've really outdone yourself this time, Princess. Bravo.

"That was so amazing," she says. "Wow."

Second thing. Here it is. I'm saying it.

"You dirty liar. I saw you take your birth control the other night. I didn't see you last night, but I'm pretty fucking sure you took it."

She bites her bottom lip and looks up and away from me. When she looks back, she bats her eyelashes. This is like The Fast and the Furious, but with eyelashes right here.

I think I lied before. I don't know. I'm pretty sure I could get another erection if she keeps this up, though. Who the fuck knew that eyelashes were sexy as fuck? I sure didn't. Not before now, at least.

"Did I?" she asks, coy, feigning innocence. "Whoops! I must have forgotten."

"You didn't forget shit!" I tell her. Seriously, real talk, she knew exactly what she was doing. "Holy fuck, you're dangerous."

"Well, I can't get pregnant *now*, Ethan!" she says, slapping my shoulder. "Seriously, I've got to finish college first. After, though..." She trails off, and offers me a sly, shy smile.

"Don't even fucking tempt me," I tell her. "I'll go to your graduation and drag you off right after you go up on stage and get your diploma, then fuck the shit out of you in a room for a week just to make sure I've done the job right."

"Promise?" she asks.

And it's those fucking eyelashes again! Seriously, what's up with that?

"Princess, you need to calm down here," I tell her. Someone has to say it, so I guess it should be me.

"Do you like it, though?" she asks. "Was it sexy?"

"Sexy as fuck, no doubt about it," I tell her.

"It's soon, though, huh?" she asks. "I know that, too. I don't want to rush anything, Ethan, but... I do want to have babies some day. I just want to finish college, too. I'm a good girl, remember?"

The way she says it... yeah, definitely makes my cock twitch. Round three? Nah, not yet. Give me a little more time, and maybe.

"I don't know what the fuck kind of good girl you are," I say. "Never met a good girl who says dirty things like that. What was with the whole 'Oh, if you cum in me when I'm cumming, I'll definitely get pregnant' thing? Is that true?"

"Maybe, kind of? It's supposed to be, but it's not like it's completely necessary or anything. I guess it just helps, or that's what I've heard."

"You used it against me, Princess. You said that just to make me cum. It worked. Good fucking job." I shake my head and sigh, pretending to be disappointed or upset or something. I have no idea.

"You liked it!" she says, kissing my cheek. "Can we do stuff like that more?" she asks. "I like pretend roleplaying. It's fun. Did you like when I was telling you no, that you couldn't?"

"Yeah," I say. Fuck yeah, actually. "Just... if you really don't want me to do something, tell me, alright? I'll stop. I don't want to force you into anything."

"You don't," she says, kissing me quick on the lips. "Never. Not even once. I really like that, Ethan. I feel like you're always careful and gentle with me, even when we're being rough."

That's a first. I don't know if anyone's ever said that to me. I guess they might have thought it, because, yeah, I try to be a considerate guy, but I think Ashley's the first girl who ever thought I was careful or gentle. Honestly, she's probably the first person who's ever thought that.

If I have my way, she's going to be the last, too. No more. I'm done. I've got all I need right here, sitting in my lap, impaled on my cock. She's enough.

To be completely fucking honest, she's probably more than enough. Seriously, this girl's a freak.

"I love you," she says, grinning at me with her lips and her eyes and her entire fucking soul. Fuck, she's beautiful.

"Yeah, I love you, too, Princess," I say. I hope I'm grinning at her with everything, too, every single fucking part of me. All of it.

7 - Ashley

ETHAN PUTS IN A FEW MORE quarters and this time we shower for real. I don't know if it's just a shower, though. We're close. Ethan runs his hands over my body, cleaning and washing me, but it's more than that, too. It's not inherently sexual, but it's...

It's nice. It's intimate and close and loving, and it's everything I could have ever hoped to have. It's something I never really knew existed before now. I didn't know relationships could be like this. I didn't know that I could feel this way. I didn't even know this was possible.

I didn't know that I could ever fully enjoy sex the way I do with Ethan. I knew it was supposed to be an enjoyable thing, and that it was supposed to feel good, but it's different with him. I feel completely uninhibited, relaxed and like I can be myself.

It's not like I'm that much different. I still want to get good grades, and I still think some of the things that Ethan and I do together are a little, um... they are not things I probably would have done before we started our stepbrother with benefits relationship. They aren't bad, though. It's nothing bad or wrong or anything I should be ashamed of.

It's an expression of myself and my hopes and dreams and desires. I guess you can say that what we just did, when I told him I wasn't on birth control even though I was, um... that was kind of kinky and I might be a sex freak. Maybe I am, too! But that's alright.

I like to think that was an expression of myself, too, though. Of my hopes and dreams. I like to think that what I was really trying to say is that I love Ethan so much and that I want to be with him, not just for now, and not just for the summer, but for a long time. Forever. The ultimate, inevitable expression of *"together"* to me is having a family.

Also, I liked that Ethan got even more aroused when I told him I could get pregnant. I mean, yes, it felt really good, and he was most certainly a sex-crazed man on a mission right then, but I liked that it didn't worry him. I think he probably knew that it was just a game, but I also think that he would have done the exact same thing if it wasn't a game. He wouldn't have regretted it, either.

I know this is strange, and I'm not going to rush into anything, believe me! But... I think Ethan would be a really good father. I don't know exactly why. There's a lot of reasons, really. He's a good person, no matter how much of a bad boy he thinks he is. Yes, he's a bad boy, too, but sometimes we need a little bad boy inside us.

Um... I want Ethan's big bad boy inside me, but... oh my God I really just thought that, didn't I? Eek...

When we finish washing up, which is a lot of fun, I help Ethan dry off. And by that I mean I take his towel and I pretend to dry him off at first, but then it's really just an excuse to stroke his partially erect cock. I can't even believe he's managing that much.

Really, Ethan? *Really?*

"If you keep that up, you better be willing to finish what you're starting, Princess," he says, his cock twitching in my hand under the towel.

I pull my hand away and toss the towel at him.

"Ugh!" I say. "Is that all you think about, Ethan Colton? Seriously!"

"You make it really fucking easy to think about," he says, smirking at me. "Fuck, look at that perfect fucking ass of yours. Bend over and give me a peek at your perfect as fuck pussy."

I shake my butt at him, teasing him. He smacks my ass in response. Pretending to bend over to reach for my clothes, I really just want to give him a show. A peek, as he said, at my... *my perfect as fuck pussy.*

"Mmm, yeah, that's it," he says.

Before I know it, Ethan is behind me. His hand caresses along my ass, soft at first, but then he squeezes hard. I stand up, but he puts his other hand on my back, keeping me bent over.

"You've been a naughty girl, Princess," he says. "I'm going to have to punish you."

"What?" I ask, curious and confused.

"You said you liked when I spanked you before, right? Yeah, well..."

He moves his hand back and smacks my ass. It's not too hard, but I can definitely feel it. The sound echoes through the shower stall, and it seems even louder now that the water's turned off.

"Ethan!" I say, hissing at him. "You--"

But apparently he doesn't care! He spanks me again, and then once more. After that he circles his hand around the curves of my ass before dipping his fingers between my legs. And, um... well, they're dipped elsewhere, too.

He presses two fingers into my slit, almost sending me off balance. He steadies me and waits for me to press my hands hard against the bench beneath me before easing his fingers out and then pushing them back in.

"I love how you're always ready for me," he says. "I love how fucking responsive you are for me, Princess. I love sliding my fingers inside you and watching you squirm."

"Do it," I say, breathy. "I dare you."

"You really are a naughty girl, aren't you?" he says, grinning and shaking his head. "Alright then. Desperate times call for drastic action."

"Um...?"

Ethan pulls me up and then spins me around. Before I realize exactly what's going on, I'm sitting on the bench next to our clothes. He pulls my legs apart, giving him an open show of everything in between. Instinctively I try to close my legs at first, but he keeps them pushed open.

"Close your eyes," he says. "I'm going to spank you again."

I close my eyes, but I don't realize at first, um...

Really, how's he going to spank me when my butt is most definitely sitting on the bench?

I realize how he intends to enact this sensual punishment a few seconds later, though.

It's soft, much lighter than when he spanked my ass, but his hand gently smacks against my pussy. It's, um... this is much more sensitive and provocative, too, though. I didn't realize what he was going to do at first since my eyes were closed, but as soon as I feel the thrumming, throbbing sensation rippling through my clit, my eyes jolt open in surprise.

Oh my God, that was...

Strange? Sensitive, definitely. Really sexy, to be honest. It... it was a lot, and if it was any harder I think it would have been too much, but as it is...

Wow. I stare at Ethan, mouth open, wide-eyed. He stares right back at me, then he smacks my pussy again. I'm ready for it this time, and a part of me is maybe waiting for it, and...

He slides his fingers up and down, teasing across the curves of my feminine folds. He slips a finger inside of me, then another, pushing in and out. Then he smacks my pussy lightly again.

I feel it. It's so strange. I don't think this is a regular orgasm. It's just small and minor, but very... twitchy? It's hard to explain. My pussy clenches of its own accord, refusing to acknowledge anything I think it should be doing. My clit spasms and throbs under Ethan's palm, and he rubs a little, side to side, goading it on. My eyes roll into the back of my head a little and all I see is bright and white.

"Yeah," Ethan says, coming up to kiss my cheek and then nibbling lightly on my earlobe. "That's my good girl, Princess."

Mmm... yup... that's me... Ashley, Ethan's Little Miss Perfect, his naughty good girl. I like it.

After that, um... well, we have to leave the shower! We fully dry off and fully get dressed and... well, that's it. We leave. I feel like this is difficult, because I think it's hard for us to leave the shower. I think I could have spent all day in there with him, except we ran out of quarters. Which is bad, because we brought a lot of quarters.

I hope they have a lot of hot water here. I'm kind of worried about that, actually. I mean, yes, it'll come back, refill, or however it works here, but by the time we were finished, the hot water was more warm than anything else, and...

"Hey!" my mom says, waving to us from the road heading to the showers. It's a decent distance away, but not that far. She's got her own change of clothes, and my stepdad is right next to her with his clothes.

"You two weren't showering this entire time, were you?" Ethan's dad asks.

"Wait, what?" my mom asks. "Were you, really? Huh!"

"Um..." I refuse to answer! I will not incriminate myself!

"Ashley's got a lot of hair," Ethan says. "Takes forever to wash."

"That's funny," my mom says. "Seems like she washes it quick on her own. I wonder what's different now?"

"Um..." I refuse! I won't!

"I understand," Ethan's dad says, smirking. "Her mom has a lot of hair, too. Might have to take our time washing that, don't you think, honey?"

"Oh, we definitely might have to do that," my mom says, grinning at him.

My mom. *That's my mom.* Ugh! Seriously?

I give her a look. That look! She just shrugs at me, feigning innocence. I'm not even buying that, Mom. Not even close.

Ethan gives his dad a thumb's up, though. What the heck! Really, Ethan? Ugh...

"Oh, Caleb was looking for you two," my mom says. "He said something about, um... he taught Gilgamesh how to shake hands, I think? Who's Gilgamesh?"

"The dog," Ethan says, sighing. "Blame Ashley. I didn't come up with that name."

"Does that make Ethan 'Enkidu' then?" my stepdad asks.

I laugh. A lot. Oh no! Is Ethan my wild man? Yes, probably.

"Who's Enkidu?" my mom asks.

"Yeah, I have no clue, either," Ethan says.

"It's a long story," Ethan's dad says, grinning at me.

"Old, too," I say. "One of the oldest, they say."

My stepdad nods. This is fun. I didn't know he knew anything about ancient mythology, but it's nice to have a shared secret. It's kind of fun, you know? It's just a silly secret, nothing serious, but it's nice. I feel like...

I don't know. I feel like we're closer. All of us. Not just myself and Ethan, but I feel closer with my mom, too, and now I feel closer with Ethan's dad, also. And I think Ethan feels the same way. I think we all do. I think we all are.

This is good. This is a great camping trip, and it's only just started. There's more. There's going to be a lot more.

"It's from the first known written story," Ethan's dad says to my mom. They're walking again, heading onwards to the showers. "*The Epic of*

Gilgamesh. Enkidu was kind of like Gilgamesh's rival and enemy at first, but then they became friends. It's an interesting story, but hard to compare to anything today. It's different."

They go into the showers, leaving us to ourselves. Before they vanish behind a closed shower stall door, my mom waves to us both.

"We'll see you two soon!" she says. "Don't get into too much trouble."

"Yeah, you hear that?" Ethan says to me. "No trouble, Princess. Don't even try it."

"Me?" I say, acting innocent.

This isn't hard, because I'm most certainly the innocent one here! Ethan's the bad one. I don't even get into trouble. I'm very good, of course.

We start walking and play fighting about who is the troublemaker. I don't think I am, because what sort of trouble have I ever started? Ethan tries to say that I make him want to cause trouble, which means that it's my fault if he does cause trouble, and I don't think that's true. It sounds like he's just making stuff up, and I'm pretty sure he is.

Caleb is waiting for us, with Hero, too. Hero's sitting in front of Caleb. Caleb glances over at us as we walk towards him. He has an excited look on his face.

"Alright... Hero!" he says to the dog. "Shake?"

Hero gives him a funny look. He doesn't look like he's going to do anything at first. Caleb's excitement progressively dwindles, until he's mostly back to a sort of unexcited stare, but...

Then Hero holds out his paw. His tongue lolls out, too. He looks very much like a goofy dog, which I think is probably the truth.

Caleb shakes hands with Hero quick, then turns to Ethan.

"See! I'm definitely cool now, right?"

Ethan purses his lips and furrows his brow, staring hard at Caleb, saying nothing.

"You said that he only listened to cool people and he listened to me so that means I'm cool?" Caleb says.

"If you have to ask if you're cool, it means you aren't cool," Ethan says.

"What? Are you for real?"

"Sorry, kid. Better luck next time."

Caleb takes a deep breath and sighs, disappointed. It's a silly sort of disappointment, though. It makes me laugh. Ethan grins, too. Caleb smiles, and we're all back to normal. Even Hero barks, excited.

"Yeah, so," Ethan says, "What's this I hear about some girl? You've got a crush on her or something?"

"Oh, uh... she's just a friend, really," Caleb says, mumbling.

"And you really like her," I say, reaffirming what he told me the other day. "She's nice to you, isn't she?"

"Well, yeah, she's nice, but I don't think she likes me like that."

"Let's just see about that," Ethan says.

"What? What do you mean?"

"You have her number, right? Let's go call her."

"Yeah, I have her number, but... I mean, she's probably busy or something. She won't want to talk to me right now. She's got art things to do."

"Fuck, she's one of those art chicks?" Ethan asks. "I can't fucking stand them."

"She's really good!" Caleb says, defending his crush. "She's different. She doesn't take herself too seriously. It's not like she thinks she's better than everyone or anything."

"Nah, she's probably bad," Ethan says. "Actually, she's probably the worst. I hate her already."

"You don't even know her, Ethan!" Caleb says, standing tall. "She's amazing and wonderful and smart and pretty, and..."

"Fuck, man, if this girl is so amazing, why the fuck are you waiting to ask her on a date? Some other guy's going to do it before you, and then where the fuck does that leave you?"

"Uh... what?"

"I'm pretty sure she's the worst," Ethan says, nodding. "If you think she's so fucking perfect, what the hell are you waiting for?"

"It's not like she's here, though," Caleb says, wavering.

"You've got her phone number, dude! Call her ass! What the fuck?"

"I... uh... do you think I should, though?"

"What the fuck did I just say?"

"You really should!" I tell him. "I bet she's interested in you but she's shy."

"I really doubt she's shy," Caleb says. "I don't even think she knows how to be shy."

"Well, let's find out," Ethan says. "Lead the way to a phone or something. We'll help you out. If she is the worst, don't say I didn't warn you, though. I'm not taking the blame for this."

"She's not the worst, Ethan! She's the best!"

They keep fighting and arguing even while Caleb leads us to a log cabin a little bit away from the front office area. I laugh and follow along. Sneaky, very sneakily... I reach for Ethan's hand. He notices, and he grabs my hand in his, holding tight. We walk like that, hand in hand, while Caleb begins to tell us all of the amazing things he likes about Scarlet.

8 - Ashley

The campground owner's cabin is small, but nice. Caleb opens the door and we step inside, immediately entering an open living room. It takes up most of the first floor, and goes all the way up to the ceiling of the second. Past a partial wall at the far end, I spot a little kitchen nook area.

"Uh, this is it, here," Caleb says, kind of showing us around.

Mostly he just waves his hands in the vicinity of the living room, which is basically just a couch, a big screen TV in front of that, and I think there's a bathroom in the back? It looks nice and rustic, but it's very simple, too.

"Yeah, house, whatever," Ethan says. "Where's the phone, kid? We going to call this girl or what?"

"I was trying to be polite!" Caleb says, glaring at Ethan.

"It's a very nice house, Caleb," I say, hoping to defuse the situation.

"It is pretty cool," Ethan says. "We can hang out here later or whatever. With your new girl- friend. Let's call her first and get her here, then we can figure the rest out. I like your couch, dude. Looks like a great place to pretend to watch a movie and then make out with a girl."

Caleb was still glaring at Ethan at first, ready to say something in defense of... whatever Ethan said, but now he's pale and he keeps glancing to his feet, then the couch, then strange sidelong looks at Ethan.

"Um... I really doubt she's going to come here, though," Caleb says. "She's a few hours away. And I don't think she's going to be my girlfriend, Ethan. Not just like that. There's more to it, isn't there? I can't just ask her to watch a movie and then... then... uh... kiss her? On the couch?"

I kind of agree with Caleb, but Ethan apparent- ly doesn't.

"What the fuck, why not?" Ethan asks.

"Uh... because?" Caleb says.

"That's not even an answer. Seriously, you aren't really this hopeless, are you?"

"Caleb isn't like you, Ethan," I say. "Maybe he wants to take things a little slower?"

"I can take things slow," Ethan says, straight- faced.

That's when I start to laugh. I can't help it! I try to stop, but then Ethan just looks at me even more confused, and that makes me laugh more.

"Listen," Ethan says, trying to explain himself. "I've gone slow. We've only had like... maybe one or two quickies the entire time we've been doing this whole stepbrother with benefits thing and then the dating thing, too."

Caleb scrunches up his brow and stares at Ethan. "Stepbrother with benefits? What the heck?"

"It's a long story," I tell him. And then to Ethan, I say, "Ethan, this isn't about having sex fast or going slow, it's about waiting to have sex at all. Some people like to take their time and wait a few days or weeks or sometimes even months. I know that sounds crazy, but..."

Ethan's eyes get wider at the mention of *days*, and they progressively grow wider still when I say *weeks*, and then *months.* He looks completely confounded and disbelieving in all of this. I just shake my head at him and sigh.

"You're joking, right? Who waits months?" Ethan asks. Seriously, he doesn't believe me! "Yeah, I mean, if you're a Catholic priest or something, I guess."

"Catholic priests don't have sex at all, Ethan! They take vows!"

"What the fuck, I know they take vows, but that's, uh... it's not forever... it's..."

"It's forever," I tell him. "*Forever* forever. That's the entire point."

"That's weird," he says. "I don't even understand."

"You're weird," I say. "Now leave Caleb alone and let him take his time if he wants to. Maybe he needs to feel comfortable before he makes out with Scarlet."

Ethan keeps shaking his head and mumbling to himself, something about not even understanding or not being able to figure any of this out. I don't think I'm supposed to laugh, but I do. It's like his entire reality has been shattered, except I'm pretty sure Ethan's the only one who could ever have believed in this sort of reality in the first place.

I go up to him and give him a hug to reassure him. "It's fine," I say. "I don't expect you to take any vows of celibacy."

"It's just... you watch those movies, right?" he says. "Horror movies in the woods, where there's campgrounds. There's plenty of them. Scary shit right there, but... usually I'm fine... this is scary, though, Princess."

"Oh, poor baby," I say, squeezing him close to me. I think that's what Ethan needs right now; breasts pressed tight against him to remind him that the world isn't filled with sexless horrors. "It's alright. Just remember what we did in the shower. Don't think about anything else."

That's apparently a really bad thing to say to my boyfriend with benefits over here, because now I can feel his growing erection pressing tight against me. To make matters worse, Ethan grabs my ass and squeezes tight, pulling me even closer.

"Ethan!" I hiss. "Um, Caleb's right there?"

"Caleb!" Ethan says, snapping out of it. "Hey, let's go call that girl?"

"Are you two alright?" Caleb asks, giving us a funny look. "What did you mean before about the shower? I thought you said you were just going to take a shower, Ashley? Nothing else, uh... wait..."

"We were just taking a shower, Caleb!" I shout.

"Yeah, Caleb," Ethan says. "Fuck, man, can't you focus here? We've got to call that girl. Where's your phone?"

9 - Ethan

THE PHONE'S UPSTAIRS, which I guess is cool. Easier and more private or something. Caleb shows us the way, and we climb the stairs. There's two loft-style bedrooms up here, one on either side of the cabin, with a walkway between them. Just outside the bedrooms there's a really cool looking bannister or balcony or whatever the fuck you want to call it. You can look down into the living room from here. Kind of a small place, but it's got some serious character.

For real, this is a great place to bring a girl to impress her. If I can't get this kid laid by the end of the week, I don't even know what to say.

Also, seriously? Seriously... there's people who wait months to have sex? How fucked up is that? Why didn't anyone tell me this before? Crazy, that's what that is.

I can't even think about it. I need to stop. It's horrifying. Campground horror movie scary. How is that even possible?

Caleb opens the door to his bedroom and Ashley slips in. There's... not much going on here. A bed, and a desk in the corner. The phone's on the desk, so that's good. It's one of those old kinds, though. Wow, this place is ancient or something. I saw a rotary phone in some museum for a field trip in elementary school way back when, and this is almost like that. Caleb's phone is cordless, so I guess he's got that going for him. Does it even work? It's plugged in, I think, so I guess so?

Fuck. This is going to be harder than I thought.

I go take a seat on the bed and pull Ashley next to me. We bounce a little. Caleb stares at us like we're doing something scandalous together. You can stop staring now, kid. I'm not going to fuck her when you're in the room. I mean, yeah, if you want to go outside and close the door behind you, I'll see if I can break your headboard with Ashley's help, but otherwise, uh...

We've got shit to do! Important shit. I don't even know why I'm doing this. I'm only helping him out because Ashley asked me to. Yeah, that's it.

Nah, Caleb's alright. A little weird, but he could be cool.

Caleb sits at the desk and stares at the phone, but he doesn't pick it up.

"What's wrong?" Ashley asks. "Are you nervous?"

"Yeah, but... is the dog going to be alright outside?" Caleb asks.

"Fuck," I say. Wow. Seriously, this dog.

"The dog's fine, Caleb!" Ashley says to him, firm. "Ethan found him in the woods, so I think he can handle himself playing around the campground, don't you?"

"Yeah, I guess..."

Wait. I know what this is. It's a thing I don't really do, because there's no time like the present, but I've heard about it. Procrastinating? People say something about procrastinating from doing their homework or whatever, too. I never understood that. I just don't bother doing it in the first place. I do it now, because of football and I need to keep up my grades for that, but that's besides the point.

You either do stuff or you don't do stuff. Don't make up excuses. Excuses are boring. Nobody likes that shit.

"Listen, here's how this is going to go," I tell him. This is my game plan. As quarterback for the football team, it's my job to be a play caller, and this is basically the same thing, right? "You pick up this phone." I reach over and pick it up for him. "You dial the--" I stare at the phone for a second. "Is this thing for real?"

"Uh, no?" Caleb says. "It's a decoration, actually. I was just going to use my cellphone."

With that, he shifts on the chair and reaches into his pocket, pulling out his phone, showing it to me.

I stare at the phone in my hand. Yeah, uh... yeah. I toss it back onto the desk and begin anew. This is an audible, guys, new play, calling it out on the fly. Adjust your positions and let's do this.

"Alright, so call her," I say.

Caleb taps some stuff, finds her number, dials. I can hear the phone ringing from here.

"It's ringing," Caleb says. "Now what?"

"Ask her on a date? It's not that hard, dude. Tell her to get her ass down here because you want to fuck the shit out of her. Say it nice, though. Don't be a dick about it."

Ashley stares at me with a mix of shock and amusement. She's trying not to laugh, biting her bottom lip. I don't see what's so funny. I'm helping our friend Caleb out here. This is no laughing matter, Princess.

Caleb's even worse. He's not laughing, he's just staring, shocked. His mouth drops and his eyes widen. The phone stops ringing. I can hear a little, and it's some girl on the other end. She says hi, but Caleb doesn't say anything.

Fuck, I broke the kid.

It's quiet, but from the phone I hear, "Caleb, is that you? I thought you were at the campground with your dad this summer."

"Caleb," Ashley whispers to him. "Say some-thing. Say hi."

"Tell her she has a nice ass, too," I whisper. Got to get the essentials in there, right?

"Seriously, Ethan? That's so dumb."

"Yeah, I mean, I don't actually know if she has a nice ass," I admit. "It never hurts to say it, though. Girls love that."

"So now I know if you tell me I have a nice butt that you're lying," Ashley says, smirking and shaking her head at me.

"Fuck, no, your ass is magnificent," I tell her. I wouldn't lie about that. No fucking way.

"Uh... Hey... Hi, Scarlet," Caleb mutters into the phone. "Yeah, I'm still at the campground, b-but I thought..."

"You were thinking about her," Ashley whispers. "Tell her that. It sounds sweet and nice, but not too much."

"You were thinking about her sexy as fuck ass," I add.

"Yeah, uh... I was... I was thinking about you," Caleb says. When I glare at him, he almost jumps out of his seat. "I was thinking about your sexy ass!"

"Caleb, did you just..." That's the girl on the phone, whoever the fuck this chick is.

"Art!" Caleb says. "I was thinking about your sexy art! It's.... it's really sexy, Scarlet. Did I ever tell you that?"

There's nothing. We've got radio silence here. Scarlet's dead, I'm pretty sure. Caleb killed her with his stupid comment. Sexy art? Who the fuck ever says that? Maybe something like he thinks she's as sexy as a painting and he wants to pin her up against his wall.

Fuck, why didn't I tell him that one sooner? That would have been a great opener. Fucking... fuck! I ruined it. I'm so sorry, Caleb. You've missed this great opportunity.

"Caleb, are you alright?" Scarlet asks. She sounds worried. I'm worried, too. How's this kid going to get laid now? Fuck if I know.

"Yeah, uh..." Caleb says, his face turning pale, then bright red, all in the span of a second.

"Give me the phone," I tell him. "I'll fix this."

He holds the phone out without thinking, kind of listless, his hand shaking a little. I snatch it from him, hold it up to my ear. Yeah, this is a little unorthodox, but I think I know what I'm doing here.

I *think* I know, but I don't actually know. I'll figure it out later.

"Hey," I say. "Who the fuck is this? Scarlet?"

"Who the fuck are you? What's going on? Did you do something to Caleb?" Fuck, this girl's got a mouth on her! I like her already. She seems...

Wait, holy shit. "Hold up. *Scarlet?* He was talking about you? No fucking way."

"Mr. Moneybags!" Scarlet shouts into the phone, laughing. "Shit, what are you doing there? Are you camping with Caleb?"

"Why the fuck does this kid have a crush on you? That's fucking weird. I can't even believe this." Yeah, holy fuck. *Scarlet?* Nah, no way. But... yeah, it's her.

I turn to Caleb. "You can't invite this girl down here," I tell him. "She's fucking crazy, bro. You'll thank me later. I'm saving your life right now."

"Ethan!" Ashley says, glowering at me.

"Put away your pouty face, Princess. For real, you don't even understand. She's insane. She'll destroy him."

"Fuck off, Ethan," Scarlet says. "Did Caleb tell you he wanted me to come down? He's never invited me to go camping. I just figured he didn't want me to hang out with him there. It's cool, really. I understand."

"Yeah, he--"

I don't get to say more than that. I don't get to save Caleb from himself, because he tackles me, grabs the phone from me, and then practically screams into it.

"Scarlet! Do you want to hang out this summer at the campground with me!"

Yeah, this isn't even a question. He's just yelling at her. Probably turns her on, too. Scarlet's weird.

She's cool, though. I like her. Would be fun if she came down to the campground. I wouldn't mind hanging out with her. Uh...

Ashley's staring at me. She looks mad. "What's up, Princess?" I ask her.

"Who's this Scarlet girl, Ethan?" she asks.

"Huh? Scarlet is Scarlet? She's got some tattoos. Paints pictures and shit."

"And...?"

And what? What the fuck am I missing here?

"What, you will?" Caleb says, surprised. "Yeah, uh... I can text you the address. Can you get down here? I could go pick you up if you want, if you don't know how to--"

Scarlet laughs. She does have a nice laugh. Just kind of commands your attention, makes you look at her. Maybe that's how she caught Caleb in her trap. He seems like the kind of guy who would fall for something like that.

Shit. I've got to warn him before it's too late. How much time do I have?

"I think I can figure it out, Caleb," she says, with a lilt of laughter in her voice. "It's only a couple hours, right? I can come down today if that's cool with you. Actually it's been kind of boring here lately. There's a lake there, right? I'll bring my bathing suit."

"Cool!" Caleb says, excited. "Yeah, there's a lake. Uh... you can stay here if you want. With us. Me and my dad, I mean. My bed's big enough for two or we have a couch or the floor or..."

Whoa! Yeah, he just said that. Casual as fuck, too. Just invites this crazy girl to sleep in his bed, no fucks given whatsoever. Maybe I underestimated him. That was good, too. Real smooth. I approve.

"Cool," Scarlet says. "Yeah, we'll figure it out. I'd love to come. I'll pack and leave in a few. I'll see you soon. Tell Ethan to fuck off for me, alright? Don't let him be a dick to you."

"Fuck you, too, Scarlet," I say.

Obviously she can hear me because she starts to laugh. Nah, but, seriously, fuck her. She's fucking crazy.

Fuck.

Caleb hangs up the phone and he looks like he's in a daze. I don't blame him. Scarlet's insanity has taken him over. He's screwed. Poor kid.

Ashley's still staring at me, though. I really don't get it. What's up? What am I missing?

"Is she... is..." Her words sound, uh... I don't even know. For real, what did I do wrong now?

"What's wrong, Princess?" I ask.

"Did you sleep with her, Ethan?" Ashley asks, hushed. "Is she one of the girls that you...?"

10 - Ashley

DON'T LIKE THIS! I really really don't. I don't like it one bit, not at all, never, not even a little.

I thought it'd be nice to help Caleb, and I guess it is nice because Scarlet is coming down here now, but... how does she know Ethan? That's the part I don't like. What if she's coming here because she wants to see Ethan again?

They were yelling at each other. It sounds sort of playful, I guess. It's hard to say. Ethan has that affect on girls, and I was witness to more than a few ended flings that involved a lot of yelling. Mostly it was the girl yelling at him, but still. That doesn't make it any better or anything.

So... yup, I just asked him, and I don't even feel bad about it. I'd ask him again, too. This is important.

"Wh-what?" Ethan stammers, staring at me like I'm crazy.

I'm not the crazy one here, Ethan! I know what sort of reputation you have! Or what reputation you had, but you better not have a reputation anymore, not ever again. You're just mine and only mine and I... I won't stand it! I won't stand for any of the stuff!

I think I'm telling him this. Not with words but my eyes. Uh huh. Yup, I glare at him, super serious.

It really is, though. I... I just want to... I don't know... I don't think I like this...

"You had sex with Scarlet?" Caleb asks, staring wide-eyed and open-mouthed at Ethan. And then, um...

Honestly I really can't even believe this happened, but, yes, it happens.

Caleb stands up, jumps at Ethan, and punches him, then tries to straddle him on the bed so he can keep punching him.

It's not actually as bad as it sounds, though. Yes, Caleb punched Ethan, but Ethan looks confused at first, just sort of taking it. It looks kind of painful, but Ethan seems unphased. When Caleb tries to pin Ethan to the bed so he can keep punching him, Ethan flips him around, pushes him down, and holds him at arm's length.

"Are you trying to make me kick his ass, Princess?" he asks. "Why would you say something like that?"

"I need to know if you did or not," I tell him, but by the way he's looking at me, I think I might have made a mistake...

Caleb keeps flailing his arms and kicking his feet, but it's not doing much. Ethan's just kind of standing there, hand on Caleb's chest, shrugging it off.

"Caleb, you goon," Ethan says, loud enough to break through the shield of rage surrounding the boy on the bed. "I've never had sex with Scarlet. No sex, no fucking. Not even a blowjob or a kiss. No handjob, either. That's fucking weird, man." Then he decides to incriminate himself. "She does have that tongue ring, though. I've heard good things about stuff like that."

Caleb started to calm down, but now he's glaring. I'm also glaring. We both glare at Ethan. *Glare!*

"You two need to calm the fuck down," he says. "That was a joke. For real."

"So she doesn't have a tongue ring?" I ask.

Is that true about tongue rings? Should I get one, maybe? I don't know if I can. It might look strange on me. Can I still be a good girl if I have a tongue ring? Will people think less of me? Um...

I mean, in the bedroom, it's fine, because it's just us, just Ethan and I, but I don't want to tell anyone about that. I don't want them to see my tongue ring and... that's private! It's...

Alright, so maybe I won't get a tongue ring. Or maybe a small one? Can I hide it? Hm...

"She has a tongue ring," Ethan admits. "But... that's not what I meant."

I glare again. Caleb glares, too. Ethan tries to glare back at the both of us, but it's two on one and we win, we outglare him. He loses. He definitely loses!

"Listen," Ethan says, backing up and leaving Caleb on the bed. "Scarlet is... she's not bad... she's pretty nice if you're into insane crazy girls, but, for real, Caleb, she's insane and crazy. Why would you like a girl like that? She's too much for you. She'll eat you alive, dude."

"She only gets into trouble sometimes," Caleb says, mumbling.

"Look, if I'm a bad boy, she's like... the same, but a girl."

Oh no. I mean, I knew a little about this before, but I don't know if I really thought about it that well.

"So, um... wait..." I say, trying to think this through. "She's rough around the edges, but sweet and nice to those who are important to her, and she gets into trouble sometimes but secretly she means well?"

"Who the fuck are you talking about?" Ethan asks. "No, that's not it at all."

"That's exactly it!" Caleb says. "Do you know her, too, Ashley?"

11 - Ashley

ETHAN AND I LEAVE the cabin shortly after the phone call with Scarlet. Caleb's dad came home and needed help with something around the campground.

"I hope everything works out," I say to Ethan as we walk away.

I'm not sure where we're going, we're just walking. I spot my mom and Ethan's dad just coming out of the shower, too. They don't see us, but my mom starts laughing and teasing Ethan's dad. My stepdad smiles and laughs, too. They have a lot of fun together, and it's nice seeing my mom happy. I don't think she was ever unhappy, or not quite, but I think it's different to be happy when you're with someone you're in love with compared to just being happy on your own or happy with your friends and family.

That's how I feel, at least. I feel different being happy with Ethan.

I reach out and take his hand in mine and he doesn't stop me. I smile and swing our hands back and forth, just out in the open. Anyone can see us, and it feels nice to be free to do something like this.

Then I remember Scarlet...

"Ethan," I say, looking over, trying to look very stern and serious. I don't know if I do a good job, because Ethan just looks at me funny.

"What's up?" he asks.

"I need to know what your relationship is with Scarlet," I say. Yes, that's a good way to word this.

Or maybe not. "What are you talking about? I don't have a relationship with Scarlet. We're sort of friends, I guess?"

"Being friends is a relationship, too," I say.

He just makes a face and shrugs. "Yeah, sure, I guess?"

"Do you find her attractive?" I ask.

"Listen, Scarlet's attractive, but she's also crazy, so any bonus points she gained for being attractive are instantly lost because she's crazy."

"What about the tongue ring?" Yes, ask him about the tongue ring now. This is the important question.

"Uh... what about her tongue ring?"

Ugh. Really, Ethan?

"Do tongue rings really make it nice?" I ask. "For um... things..." I sneak closer to him so I can whisper in his ear. "For blowjobs? If I had a tongue ring, would you like it?"

"I guess?" he says. "That's what I've heard. Guys say that it feels better, but to be completely fucking honest with you, Princess, I'm pretty sure a blowjob always feels good. My idea of a good time definitely involves my cock in your mouth. Or your pussy. Your hand. We can get creative here if you want. I'm open to more ideas."

Alright, mouth, pussy, hand... wait, *more* ideas? Um...

"What else is there?" I ask. "I think you just named everything."

"Holy shit, no way. Breasts? Aw yeah... anal sex, too. Some guys are into feet, but that's not really my thing. There's also when you hold a girl's thighs tight together and just kind of thrust between them. Not inside her, right? But between her thighs. Not really sure what the point is with that one, but I guess if you angle it right then my cock's going to press against your clit every time I thrust forward, so..."

Ooohhhh, hmmm... I try to picture it in my mind, and while it seems kind of strange at first, I can definitely see the appeal. Maybe we can...

Wait! I'm getting distracted by Ethan's bad boy ways.

"Stop distracting me!" I tell him. "We were talking about tongue rings and how Scarlet is attractive and she has a tongue ring and I can't deal with this Ethan, you need to..."

To what? I don't know. That's what I'm trying to figure out.

"You don't even have to worry about Scarlet," he tells me. "She's cool, and I hang out with her sometimes, but most of the time it just ends up with us doing stupid shit and getting into trouble, or almost getting into trouble. I think it's a bad idea for her to come here, because who fucking knows what's going to happen? Probably the entire forest gets burned down or something. It's not like she's a pyromaniac or anything, but bad things happen when Scarlet is around."

"Bad things happen when you're around," I point out. "Also, that's what I'm worried about, Ethan. The trouble part you mentioned. I... I don't want you to do things with her that will get you in trouble with me..."

I think maybe that's an awkward way to say it, but, there, I said it.

"I promise not to burn the forest down," Ethan says, completely missing the point of what I'm saying.

"That's not what I meant," I say. "I mean, um... I don't... you can't have sex with her or anything, Ethan."

"Would you cut that shit out?" he says. "Princess, we've got rules. I think that's one of the rules, isn't it? I'm serious about these. I'm not going to fuck around."

"I know, it's just..."

I know, but I don't know. Yes, we have rules, but the entire idea behind a bad boy is that he doesn't exactly follow the rules? I don't even know why I feel this way, it's just the way Ethan was talking to Scarlet on the phone. They seem more casual. They seem...

Ethan swirls me around, then picks me up, just like that. I'm straddling his waist and his hands are cupping my butt, holding me like that. Our noses touch, my face so very close to his. He presses forward and kisses me, holding me like that. Instinctive, I wrap my hands behind his neck and kiss him back.

I don't know why I'm doing this. To be honest, I don't even fully realize what I'm doing. Then it all kind of hits me at once and... oh my God we're standing out in the middle of the front of the campground, Ethan's hands are holding my butt, I'm basically straddling him in the air, and we're making out.

Also, Hero decides right then to come up and start barking at us.

"Fuck you, Hero," Ethan says to him. "I'm kissing my girlfriend here. Don't be a dick."

"Ethan, he's a dog," I say. "He's not being a dick."

"He's trying to cockblock me. That's being a dick in my book."

"We can't have sex right out here in the open, so there's no cockblocking going on," I say.

"Oh yeah? You think we can't?"

Um... well... yes, I did think that, but now I'm not so sure? I jolt my head side to side quick to see if anyone is watching us. There's a few people off in the distance and I think they look our way, but mostly we're just by ourselves.

There's more, though. It's fun to get excited like this, but there's more, too. We're just starting our relationship, and I just... I need to talk to him. That's one of our rules, too, isn't it?

"I'm just nervous," I tell him, truthful.

He gives me a confused look. "I was just kidding, Princess. I'm not going to fuck you right here. I'd drag you to the showers or something. Speaking of... I think we forgot our clothes..."

I laugh. "Yeah, um... we should go get those."

"Yeah," he says. "Let's talk, too. I promise not to try and seduce you for at least ten minutes. That's about as long as I can hold off, though."

We go to get our clothes, but this isn't even normal. Ethan carries me exactly like he's already holding me, his hand under my butt, my legs wrapped around his waist as he lifts me higher. I hug his neck tight to keep myself from falling, and I'm pretty sure this is exactly what he wanted to happen. My breasts practically smother his face, and he doesn't even try to pretend he doesn't enjoy it.

"This is going to be the longest ten minutes of my life," he mutters.

"Be good!" I tell him, bopping him on the head.

"Yes, ma'am," he says, but then he presses his nose between my breasts and shakes his head side to side.

"Not like that!"

12 - Ethan

THIS IS SERIOUS, I GUESS. I understand that, alright? It's not like I'm a complete idiot here. I know that sometimes you need to do things like talk and all of that. Yeah, so I haven't exactly been in a regular relationship before, but I still know how to talk to people. I might be better at fucking than talking, but with Ashley I want to be good at both.

I get where she's coming from, too. I don't blame her for worrying. I've kind of fucked up a lot in my life, and she has a right to get nervous about me potentially fucking up again. To be honest, I'm sure I'm going to fuck something up sometime, because, uh... I'm only eighteen. Almost nineteen now. Holy shit, I'm getting old.

But, yeah, I might do something stupid, but I'm going to try and do this like my dad does.

Business junk, right? Calculated risks, but nothing that's going to hurt people or destroy me. Uh... maybe that's how that works? Fuck, what about the stock market? Yeah, those guys think they're playing the stocks game fine, but then they lose all their money and who the fuck knows what happens after that?

I think I'd rather be poor than hurt Ashley, though. I'd rather lose everything else I have before I lose her. We've got rules, and I plan to follow them. To be fair, I think they're pretty easy to follow. Especially rule number eleven. Did I eat her out yet today? Nah, but it's a rule, and...

Calm the fuck down, Ethan! We're talking here.

Or, we're about to.

We go into the shower stall to get our clothes and I sit down on the bench next to her. It's kind of private in here, but without the shower to distract us, everything we say echoes off the walls and bounces back to us, sounding more serious and important. You can't just say something in here, you have to listen to yourself say it, too. There's a difference.

I'm not like that, anyways. Some guys say shit to girls and they don't mean it. I try not to do that. If I did, I never meant to. I don't know if that makes it better, because I've still hurt a lot of people, but I tried to be upfront with them from the start.

I'm going to be upfront with Ashley, always..

"It's rule number ten," she says after a little while of silence. "That one was that you can't sleep with other girls while we're doing what we're doing, but that was the stepbrother with benefits for a week thing, I think."

"It's not," I tell her, steady. "It's not just for a week, Princess. I won't do that ever. Just you and me, alright?"

"Yes, but..." She hesitates. "What about a three-some? Like, me and you and then another girl, too?"

Holy fuck, I'm dead. Is she crazy? This girl is going to kill me. I seriously almost die from choking. Where the fuck did that come from?

"Ethan! Are you... Ethan, are you alright?" She slaps me on the back, for all the good it does. I'm not choking on food over here, Princess, I'm choking on your words.

"We're not having a threesome," I say. Just need to get that out of the way right now. "I'm not even going to try and stretch these rules, Princess. No fucking way. No theoretical or technical or whatever the fuck else kind of bullshit some guys might try to use."

"Are you sure?" she asks me, straight-faced.

I don't know how she can look so serious after what she just said. Maybe Scarlet isn't the only crazy girl I know. Fuck, I'm screwed. They're both going to kill me in entirely different ways. Caleb better fucking get laid and fall in love or some shit, because this isn't even worth it.

"I'm going to be completely honest with you right now," I say. "You're too much, Princess. You are entirely too fucking much, and when I'm with you, the only thing I can think about is you. Like, right now, that's all I can really think about. I mean, yeah, there's other stuff sometimes, but it's always about the other stuff *and* you. A threesome? What the fuck would be the point? I'd be too distracted by you and just you, so I don't know what the fuck the other girl would be doing. Just sitting there, I guess. Not really my thing."

"It could be another guy," she offers. "A threesome doesn't just have to be with another girl, Ethan."

"There's not going to be another guy," I tell her. "If you need another guy, I'm just not doing it right."

"But there's... there's that thing, um..."

I'm conflicted, because I don't want there to be *that thing*, except the way she's murmuring and looking all shy as fuck right now is seriously turning me on, and I kind of want to know what it is.

"What?" I ask her. "What thing?"

"Um... double penetration or something? When, er... things... and..."

"Princess, I know what double penetration is," I tell her. "What the fuck kind of porn have you been watching?"

"I don't watch porn, Ethan. I'm a lady."

"A lady who likes deepthroating my cock and whispering about how she's not on birth control so if I keep fucking her she's going to get pregnant," I point out.

She blushes and buries her face in my shoulder. Holy fuck, I just want to rip off our clothes and sit her down on my cock right now, but I don't think ten minutes has passed yet. Why are you doing this to me, Princess?

"This isn't even about that," I tell her. "You're just making shit up trying to see if I'm going to break the rules or bend the rules or whatever the fuck, and I'm telling you right now that I'm not going to. Here, let's even make it a rule. How's that sound?"

"That sounds weird," she says. "That doesn't even make sense."

"It makes perfect sense," I tell her. "What rule are we on now?"

"Twenty-two, I think."

"Sure. Rule number twenty-two is that I will never break any of the rules."

"It's dumb, though," she says, laughing. "You can't make a rule about not breaking the rules, because you're not supposed to break the rules in the first place. It's kind of already a rule."

"It's a double rule now, then. It's an unwritten rule and it's rule number twenty-two."

"I guess..."

"We're going to write this shit down," I tell her. "I'm going to memorize it. I'm going to follow every fucking rule so damn hard, you don't even know, Princess."

She laughs again, then tilts her head up and kisses my cheek. "Alright," she says.

"Good," I say.

"Um... Ethan?"

"Yeah?"

"Do you want me to get a tongue ring? Because I think it could be neat, but also if someone sees I have a tongue ring they're going to think things about me, won't they? Can I hide it? How do tongue rings work."

This is complicated, but this is also my specialty. I know how to do bad things and some-times get away with it, so I can work with her here and come up with a plan of action.

"First off, it's not about me, it's about you," I say. "If you want to get a tongue ring, that's cool, though. If not, whatever. I'll gladly let you suck my cock either way, Princess. Don't even worry about that."

"Oh, you're so chivalrous and polite," Ashley says, rolling her eyes at me.

"Yeah, chivalrous as fuck. That's what every-one says," I say, grinning at her.

She just rolls her eyes again. Has it been ten minutes yet? Yeah... she's done for once that time passes. We don't even have a fucking timer, though. Shit.

"If you're worried about people finding out and, uh... thinking... things?" *What the fuck does that even mean?* "Yeah, if you're worried, then just get something else pierced. Won't be the same or have the same effect, but there's other piercings that can be sexy, Princess."

"Huh? Like what?"

"Nipples?" I offer. "Maybe your clit?"

Fuck, man... now I can't stop thinking about it. Ashley's perfect as fuck breasts, just right there. I imagine her laying on my bed, naked, a little shy blush on her cheeks, and then to top it all off, her firm nipples pierced right through with little bars. I start to fucking daydream about licking all around them, paying severe and extreme attention to her breasts, her nipples.

Some girls can cum just from that, or so I've heard. Never really had the patience for it considering I can make them cum in quite a number of other ways, but if Little Miss Perfect wants to give it a shot, I'd be willing to try it out.

I don't need another reason to lap up every fucking drop of her arousal with my tongue, either, but I'd be happy to have an excuse to pay her clit even more attention. This is kind of shaping up to be a good idea. I don't know if it's my best idea, and, really, it's up to her, but I'm down if she is.

"What about you?" she asks, interrupting my sexy daydreams.

"Uh, what?"

"Guys get things pierced for sexy stuff, too, don't they? Your tongue or your nipples or, um..."

I die. I think I die. I don't know if that's a serious turn on or a boner killer. Do I want something piercing through my cock? I am pretty fucking sure my cock is supposed to go inside things, and not have things go inside it. Mainly, it should be inside Ashley right now. I don't know why it's not.

Ten fucking minutes has to have passed by now. It just has to. Fuck...

"We'll talk about it," I tell her, smiling. "I like you just the way you are, though. Don't change for me, Princess, because you're seriously perfect already."

She blushes and smiles at me, then sneaks in quick to give me a kiss on the lips. Just a little, some tiny as fuck kiss, but it's nice. Never knew I liked little pecks and small displays of affection before, but they're growing on me. Ashley turns them into something amazing that I never knew was possible.

"You're really nice and sweet sometimes, did you know that?" she asks.

"I'm nice as fuck and sweet all the fucking time," I tell her.

"Oh, sure, alright," she says, rolling her eyes.

"Is everything alright now, though?" I ask.

"I think so, but can I ask you something?"

"Yeah, sure," I say. "Whatever you want. Ask away."

"Is Scarlet really crazy? Caleb must like her for a reason. Can we hang out with them, too? Will you introduce me to her and tell her I'm your girl-friend?"

That's... I don't even know what that is. I can't say I've ever told someone that a girl's my girl-friend before. Mostly because I haven't had a girlfriend before. Huh. It sounds kind of fun, actually? Is that weird or what?

"Yeah, I'm going to do that," I say. "I like it. I guess we can hang out with them, too. Honestly, she's not so bad."

"I bet she's really nice and amazing, and that's why Caleb likes her."

"Caleb's weird and fucked up in the head, so I can see why he's got a crush on an insane girl."

"I have a crush on someone, too," Ashley says, sneaky.

I have a feeling I know where this is going, and I like it. "Oh yeah, who?"

"You," she says, then she presses her lips to mine. Aw yeah... I definitely like it.

Unfortunately this doesn't end up going too far, because someone starts banging on the shower stall door. Then, to make matters even worse, the stupid dog crawls under and joins us. Jumps right the fuck in my lap and everything. The shower stall door isn't locked, either. Ashley's mom opens it and stands in the doorway, tall, peering at the two of us.

"What are you two doing?" she asks, narrowing her gaze.

We're not naked, so this is good. I don't have to even make anything up.

Ashley doesn't even bother making anything up.

"I was kissing my boyfriend, Mom!" she says, scrunching up her face.

"Well, get out here! We're going to lunch. There's a nice restaurant nearby that John and Caleb told us about, and I'm hungry."

"Bring the dog, too," my dad says from around the corner. "We're going to drop him off at the vet and make sure everything's alright. Hopefully we're not all covered in fleas now."

Yeah, thanks, Dad. He definitely knows how to set the mood. Hero's sitting in my lap, too, just being a fucking dog. He doesn't look like a lap dog, but I guess I'm comfortable as fuck. It's cool, I understand.

"Do you have fleas?" I ask Hero. "You better not."

Hero stares at me and starts to whine.

"I think that means he does," Ashley says.

"Why are you doing this to me? I gave you a name and everything. It's a cool as fuck name that Ashley came up with, and you just go and ruin it by having fleas? Seriously, what the fuck?"

"What's the name again?" my stepmom asks. "Oh, is it Muffins?"

Ashley and I both turn to her at the same time with a sort of *what the fuck?* look on our faces.

"Muffins?" we say at the same time.

"Chocolate Chip Muffins?" my stepmom offers.

"His name is Gilgamesh," I say.

"King of Heroes," Ashley adds with a nod.

"Alrighty then..." her mom says.

"I still like Muffins," my dad says.

This dog is going to end up with so many fucking names.

13 - Ashley

'd like to say that that's it and the rest of the camping trip goes well. It does go well, but there's a little more to it. It's... um... well, it's hard to explain. It's nothing too bad.

It's actually kind of bad.

Before we head back to our campsite to get into one of the cars so we can bring Hero to the vet and then go to lunch, Caleb and his dad show up. This is normal, of course, but...

"Oh, I almost forgot," my stepdad says. "Hey, John, would it be possible for me to use your phone? It won't take long."

"What the fuck?" Ethan says. "I thought this was a technology free trip. No phones, remember?"

Ethan's dad sighs. "We didn't bring our phones, so I think it's fine. Honestly, it'll just be a second. I need to call home and see if we got any messages at the house. I was supposed to get a call early today about some business arrangements, and I just want to make sure they're going according to plans. I'll make it quick, I promise."

Part of this settles into my mind and I vaguely think I should remember something important, but I can't quite figure it out. Why would my stepdad's business messages be important, though? Um...?

"Yeah, that's fine," John says. "The office door is unlocked, so help yourself. Caleb and I have to head out to fix something at the other end of the camp. Just make sure you close the door when you're done."

"Sure thing," my stepdad says.

We all go to the front office. I'm not sure why we all have to go, but we're all together, so why not? It's big enough for us to fit in, but just barely. Ethan's dad heads over to the desk and the phone while Ethan and I stand close, kind of cuddling, and my mom hovers by the door.

"I didn't think it was that big of a deal, but I'll put it on speakerphone so you know I'm not doing anything suspicious, alright?" my stepdad says.

Ethan shrugs. I nod. My mom laughs.

Ethan's dad dials our house number and then presses some numbers so that he can tap into our voicemail. He types the password in using the phone keys, then confirms that he wants to listen to messages.

"There are nine new messages," the robotic female voice reassures us. "Your first message is from--"

It tells us the number, then goes straight to the message. This is apparently what Ethan's dad was hoping to hear. I don't really understand it, but it sounds like it's good news. Ethan's dad smiles and nods. When the message is over, he presses a number to save it, and the voicemail voice starts to bring us the next message.

That's when it hits me, and I realize what I was worried about before. It's kind of too late now, though.

"I can't believe this," Jake's voice says via speakerphone. "I'm done trying to play nice here, Ashley. It's obvious you aren't taking me seriously. I have the pictures you texted me, plus the texts saying you're going to give your brother a blowjob. No more games, no more chances or opportunities. I was still willing to try and work something out, even after your muscle jock brother punched me at the airport, but I can see that was a waste of time. Good luck trying to figure out how to explain your screwed up incestuous brother-sister relationship to everyone at college, because I'm literally going to tell all of them. I'm going to hang up fliers, put your nude pictures on the school message board, everything. I'm going to make your life a living hell, you bitch!"

That's the end of that message. Ethan's dad stares down at the phone, confused.

"Uh... does anyone want to explain to me what that was about?" he asks.

"Nah," Ethan says, shrugging. "Just some stupid fuck being a stupid fuck."

"I agree with Ethan," my mom says. "Jake *does* seem like a stupid fuck."

"Mom!" I say. "Did you really just say that?"

"You should try it, Ashley. It's very cathartic."

Um... I think... alright, fine!

"He really is a stupid fuck," I say.

Oh, wow, that really is nice. My mom was right. Huh.

"Alright, I get it," my stepdad says. "What was he talking about with pictures and... he knows about Ethan and Ashley dating?"

"Um... he does know..." I say. "He tried to blackmail me, too, and I, um... well, Ethan followed me and then he punched Jake and told him to stay away from me."

"Apparently I didn't punch the stupid fuck hard enough," Ethan says, grunting.

We listen to the rest of the voicemail messages, but they're all from Jake. I don't know why he's so obsessed with this. It's kind of crazy and weird. I can't believe I dated him. Ugh.

"You know what?" my stepdad says afterwards, hanging up the phone. "I don't even care. Who cares? Does anyone care?"

"I don't care!" my mom says. "I think Ethan is very nice and him and Ashley are cute together."

"Aww, thanks, Mom," I say, blushing.

"I already punched the asshole," Ethan says. "Not sure I care anymore."

"I've dealt with people like him before," my stepdad says. "He's all talk. It'll blow over. By the time school starts back up for you two, he probably won't even remember anymore. Let's go back to having a nice family vacation and then a great rest of the summer, because life is short and we need to make the best of it."

I smile, and then I do something I haven't really done before. It's just something I guess I never thought about doing. I shuffle to the side and then scoot forward and I put my arms around my stepdad and give him a hug. He looks confused at first, but then he smiles wide and hugs me back.

"Thank you for understanding," I tell him.

"Not a problem, Ashley," he says. "Thank you for helping me to understand. I think you and Ethan are good for each other."

We are. I know it. Nothing can stop that from being true.

A NOTE FROM MIA

AND THAT'S THE END OF SEASON TWO!

To be honest, I got kind of carried away with this one. There were so many things I wanted to write about, because I had so many fun ideas. I realized that maybe they weren't the most important things to add, even though I thought they were fun and exciting.

I know some people aren't as interested in that, so I tried not to get too carried away, but... really, I could have probably just kept writing a ton, haha.

I also know that some people do like that, so if you are one of them, please keep reading!

I'll still be writing these extra scenes! Mostly they're a bonus, because everything is happy and fun for Ethan and Ashley, at least for now. They've still got the rest of their summer vacation to look forward to, and a little more with the camping trip. No one has to worry about Jake for at least a couple more months.

If you're interested in these bonus scenes, please definitely follow me on Facebook! I'll be posting them on the Cherrylily site and then sharing the links on Facebook, so you won't want to miss that. This will include lots of fun stuff from the summer vacation, and not just the camping trip. I'd like to do a beach scene with Ethan and Ashley when they go back home, and some more things, too.

I also maybe might include some scenes between Scarlet and Caleb... hmmmm...

The bonus scenes will be available for free and I'll be adding them every so often while I start working on the Season Three books, but also if you would like to get them all together as an e-book, that'll be in the works once I've written them all, too.

Those will be separate from the main Step-brother With Benefits storyline, though. They aren't necessary to read, they're extras. I think you'll really enjoy them, though. I'm going to call them the Stepbrother With Benefits: Summer Break Celebration! I think it sounds fun and fancy, haha.

Also, did I mention Season Three? I just did, but I'm going to mention it again.

There'll be a Season Three! It's going to take place when Ethan and Ashley go back to school, and will involve Ashley arriving back at college to some unfortunate circumstances... I think the ending part here with Jake explains a lot about how that might go. Also, though, Ethan and Ashley go to different schools. At the end of Season One, they talked about visiting each other every weekend, back and forth, but there's still going to be some long distance issues involved that I'd like to explore there.

I think it'll be interesting and I definitely hope you'll check it out. I'm going to be working on that and I hope to have the beginning available soon. Depending on when you read this, it might even be available now? That'd be neat! Once the beginning is available, I'll be working on adding new episodes just about every two weeks, so you won't have to wait long to get more. It'll be like a TV show, and I think it's fun to have a schedule like that to look forward to.

If you liked Season Two, I hope you'll review this book and all the rest of the books if you haven't already! It's fun to see what you think. Did you like the way it turned out with Ethan and his dad? I thought it was nice and sweet and happy. Also, I like Ashley's mom and her strangeness sometimes, haha. She's funny. I think Ethan's bad boy ways are wonderful, too. I'm also looking forward to seeing how things might pan out with Scarlet and Caleb...

Here's a quick secret from Season Three, but Scarlet and Caleb will be in that, too. I don't want to give away too much, but where do you think Ethan met Scarlet? He might have even run into

Caleb before the camping trip without even realizing it...

Bye for now!

$\sim$M IA

ABOUT THE AUTHOR

Mia likes to have fun in all aspects of her life. Whether she's out enjoying the beautiful weather or spending time at home reading a book, a smile is never far from her face. She's prone to randomly laughing at nothing in particular except for whatever idea amuses her at any given moment.

Sometimes you just need to enjoy life, right?

She loves to read, dance, and explore outdoors. Chamomile tea and bubble baths are two of her favorite things. Flowers are especially nice, and she could get lost in a garden if it's big enough and no one's around to remind her that there are other things to do.

She lives in New Hampshire, where the weather is beautiful and the autumn colors are amazing.

Manufactured by Amazon.ca
Bolton, ON

17937869R00079